VIDA

A MYSTERY NOVEL BY DELACORTA

That odd couple is in L.A. "Utterly contemporary,
genuinely intelligent, fresh, brash, bright
and witty, even sly."
Dallas News

A MYSTERY NOVEL BY DELACORTA

"Could have sprung full-blown from the pages of a
stoned comic book.....a surprisingly good read."
The Washington Post

A MYSTERY NOVEL BY DELACORTA

"My lemon sorbet, my California bitter
orange, my African Eskimo Pie, my volcanic
iceberg, my apple pan-Taody."
Alba on Gorodish

VIDA

A MYSTERY NOVEL BY DELACORTA

Translated from the French by
Victoria Reiter

Ballantine Books · New York

FOR JOY AND BOB

Author's Note: Most of the chapter headings
are phrases taken from *The Long Goodbye*,
by Raymond Chandler.

English Language Translation Copyright © 1985 by Summit Books, A
Division of Simon & Schuster, Inc.
Copyright © 1985 by Delacorta

Library of Congress Catalog Card Number: 85-14693

ISBN 0-345-32941-4

This edition published by arrangement with Summit Books, A Division
of Simon & Schuster, Inc.

Manufactured in the United States of America

First Ballantine Books Edition: September 1986

Rumba

THE TWA 747 LANDED AT LOS Angeles International Airport and Alba and Serge Gorodish disembarked with nothing but the clothes on their backs and a small case containing twenty-five pounds of piano scores. Even after the twenty-two-hour flight from Paris, Alba's smile was as big as the Ritz and Gorodish looked as hungry as a lion. They were going to tear up the town.

As they walked past the cocktail lounge two photographs of a smiling Marilyn Monroe seemed to bid them welcome.

"I'm dried out," said Alba. "I want a big Coca-Cola, like the ones you see kids slurping down on American TV."

They seated themselves at the bar. "I should like a bourbon," said Gorodish in his best Berlitz language-lab English.

"And a large Coke for me," added Alba.

The barmaid laughed. "Frogs, hunh? There's Coke, and then there's coke: depends how you pronounce it. You'd better say côôôôke, or people'll think you mean something else."

"Okay," said Alba, "Côôôôke."

"Any brand of bourbon in particular?"

"Let me taste the one you like best," said Gorodish who believed one could always learn from the natives.

With a Dolly Parton smile the barmaid set out a line of snifters and Gorodish found himself facing one shot each of Wild Turkey, Old Grand Dad, Jim Beam, Jack Daniel's and George Dickel.

"Whichever you like best is on me," said the barmaid.

His nymph watched admiringly as Gorodish drank the bourbon in small, eager sips.

"Well?" said the barmaid.

"I think it's either the Wild Turkey or the George Dickel."

"You've got good taste. But I'll let you in on a little secret: the best bourbon in America is called Michter's. It's hard to come by because it's made in a small distillery somewhere in Pennsylvania, in Amish country. The distillery's the oldest in the United States; it dates back to 1753 or around there."

"I'll find it and bring you back a gallon," Gorodish promised.

"Okay, sweetie, but right now I think you better eat some peanuts."

Gorodish did as she suggested, but even so, the moment he tried to slide off the stool, a picture of Gary Cooper hanging behind the bar suddenly seemed to be staring at him with three eyes. To Gorodish's knowledge Cooper had never made a movie based on the writings of Lobsang Rampa, and even though the airport was not far from Hollywood and its movie tycoons, that was still no reason for him to be seeing monsters.

"Gary Cooper's funny, isn't he?"

"Tall," Alba agreed.

They came out of the terminal and were heading toward the taxi stand when Alba let out a shriek.

"What's wrong?" asked Gorodish.

"A palm tree!"

"I think we'd better check into the first motel we can find," said Gorodish who was experiencing neuromotor difficulties. His sweaty hand gripped Alba's shoulder as he tried not to crash into the concrete pillars holding up the airport roof.

"A nap in the middle of the day?" asked Alba. "You must be smashed. Let's look around first. It's important we spend our first night here in some magical place."

"My fate is in your hands," said Gorodish; "just get me into a taxi."

The cabdriver, who looked barely old enough to drive, resembled Bob Marley, hair plaited, dreadlocks sprouting from beneath his tam. Turning down the sound blasting from the cab's six stereo speakers, he inquired as to where his passengers wanted to go.

"Hi," said Alba, "show us the town."

"You crazy, baby?"

"Yes."

"Los Angeles is four hundred fifty square miles, give or take. What, exactly, did you want to see?"

"Palm trees, the Pacific Ocean, Marilyn Monroe's house, Hollywood . . ."

"Got it," said the pseudo-Marley. Smiling engagingly, he lit up a joint that looked more like a rocket ship than a cigarette and contained enough grass to turn on half of Babylon.

Gorodish was nodding in the semitropical heat, his head bobbing up and down in rhythm to the rocking of the shock absorbers. Turning up the car stereo the driver headed toward Santa Monica as the speakers vibrated through two minutes, forty-seven seconds of Duke Ellington's "Rumba" (commissioned by Orson Welles in 1941): liquid dynamite.

A deejay, his voice filled with shadows, announced, "KKGO, all jazz, all the time."

"At least we're starting off on the right beat," said Gorodish before passing out completely.

"Your old man's wasted. I know what that's like that's why I don't do anything but good reefer."

"Listen, Bobby, if you want us to get along don't be insulting. He's not my old man; he's my man."

"Can he still get it on? He's 'round forty, isn't he?"

"What is this? You want the story of my life, or something?"

"Listen, baby, it's been a long time since I heard anythin *really* moved me. Even the Australian papers been gettin too realistic. My mama brought me up on fairy tales; I used to love them when I was a kid.

So get to it, let me hear somethin rare, somethin romantic. Take a little hit on this first: it'll help stir up your head."

He handed the joint to Alba who took three big puffs. It certainly wasn't eucalyptus. The taxi turned into a helicopter.

"Once upon a time," she began, "in a small French town, there lived a princess named Alba. She was the prettiest blonde in the galaxy. She was also thirteen, and bored. Her mother had run off with a passing knight and her father, who didn't have enough money to join a Crusade, had started to drink. To while away the time the princess shoplifted and dreamed of a Prince Charming...."

"Was she a virgin?"

"What's wrong with you? Princesses are always virgin until the night of their fourteenth birthday. At least that's what Prince Charming promised."

"Good thing it's not tonight," the driver said. "How 'bout I take care of it for you?"

"Back to our story," said Alba. "One day Prince Charming stepped off the train. He had a vaguely Mongol look about him. Love at first sight. A few weeks later we robbed a local bank, after which he swept me away to that first step toward paradise: Paris. Music. Diva. Did you see the movie?"

"*Diva*? Oh, yeah, that movie about a black opera singer and pirated tapes and drugs, right? I think it was on cable last week."

"We made some money on that, too," said Alba. "Unfortunately, right after that I stole a Rolls-Royce and it might have turned out badly if it hadn't been for Freud and Serge. A crazy man thought I was a dragonfly so he kidnapped me."

"I can see them little pink wings."

"Get serious, Bobby."

"You talkin death and violence, here?"

"Naturally, as in all fairy tales; but *we* almost always win."

"That's why I don't hardly go to the movies," said Bobby. "It's immoral, the cops always winnin. . . ."

"You aren't going to start crying, are you? After that, our passion grew ever more intense. . . ."

"I like that. Your man in the backseat: what's his story?"

"He's a great pianist, a great con man, a great lover, a . . ."

"Yeah. You told me you're still a virgin."

"I've learned to separate love and sex. Believe me, I've tried everything to seduce him. It's a good thing I don't have much longer to wait."

"You Europeans are sure strange."

"After that we found Lola, you remember, the rock star who disappeared?"

"No kidding? Lola Black? You found Lola Black?"

"Yes, and earned the reward. That's the best part of our fairy tale: not only do we meet a lot of people but we usually manage to get our hands on some cash, too. The problem is Serge is very emotional, he always winds up falling in love with the people we're dealing with. If it weren't for me he'd never remember the practical side."

"I like your story, baby. Is all that shit true?"

"Fairy tales are always true."

Ornithology

ORNITHOLOGY WAS ONE OF *the* jazz spots in Los Angeles, the latest in a series of five clubs Vida had owned to bear the name. This newest Ornithology was situated in a dark basement in the heart of Watts. According to the Los Angeles Fire Department, the room could hold one hundred twenty-five people, a clientele composed of musicians, jazz fans, whores and neighborhood pimps who usually showed up after two in the morning.

Vida had always thought of herself as culturally black, for she had been born, and had grown up, among jazz musicians.

Tonight the last customers and the young jazz trio left at about the same time. Only Sean, a medical student from USC, remained seated at the bar. Like most men he was fascinated by Vida; she, in turn, treated him with a vague tenderness untainted by illusions. Now she walked over and ran her fingers through his hair. For the last three nights she had allowed him to stay on after closing, had let him take her to breakfast at Vickman's, the restaurant in the wholesale produce market downtown, before sending him back to his termite-ridden bungalow near the campus. Although she never felt remorse at the pain she inflicted on men Vida had no desire to add Sean to the list. She, herself, had lived with pain ever since she was born, music being the one thing that had brought her even brief moments of surcease.

Seating herself at the bar, Vida poured a shot glass of bourbon. "Fine sounds tonight," she said. "They're young, but they'll make it."

"What about me?"

"You'll make it, too," said Vida.

Sean stared at the wall behind the bar. It was covered with photographs of all the great jazz musicians, some dating back to the 1930s. Most of the photographs, through the 1950s, were autographed to someone named Carla. The rest were signed "For Vida." Sean was intrigued. The woman's entire life seemed to have been devoted to jazz. It was obvious that she was adored, considered almost a goddess of music. He could sense that she had some power, some influence, over the musicians, but of what sort, and why, he could not fathom.

"Who's Carla?"

"See, there's a picture of her with Fats Navarro, and another with Mingus, and Charlie Parker, and Lester Young."

"She's beautiful."

"She was my mother."

"Is she dead?"

"She died of a combination of tuberculosis and an overdose, just six weeks before Charlie Parker."

"How old were you?"

"Eighteen. Carla started working when she was nine. It was the middle of the Depression. She began joypopping at twelve. She'd enter dance marathons; you know, people staggering around a dance floor for two or three days just to earn a couple of hundred dollars. I think she even won a few. At fifteen she went to Kansas City. Folks still talk about those days. There were fifty nightclubs in the town, city hall was corrupt, and there was more booze around than you could drink in a year of trying. You could walk down the street and go from Duke Ellington to Count Basie, from Jay McShane to the Dorseys, Buster Smith, Earl ("Fatha") Hines, Lester Young, Sarah Vaughan, Oscar Pettiford, Charlie Parker . . . just about everybody was there. There'd be jam sessions in Tasco Park just before sunrise. Carla had always lived with musicians. I was only a baby at the time but I can remember it so clearly. There were fifteen big bands playing K.C. in those days. Today there's almost nothing left. The only trace of what it used to be is Charlie Parker's grave, and the Count Basie Orchestra's opening an office."

"You went to New York after the war?"

"Yes. World War Two. Everyone was moving east so we sort of followed along."

"What about your father?"

"He was probably some musician. You want to hear something special?"

"Aren't you tired?"

"No," said Vida. "I usually play this early in the morning when I'm all alone, closing up the club. It's my mother."

"Did she make a record?"

"Sort of. You can hear her voice on one cut of this Charlie Parker album. She must have been standing near the mike."

Vida placed her favorite record on the turntable. "'One Night in Birdland,'" she said. "It was recorded during a live performance, June 30, 1950. The other musicians are Fats Navarro and Bud Powell."

The long night had honed her senses: she could clearly hear her mother's voice saying, "Come on, baby!" urging Parker on, and over the applause at the end of the number the sound of Carla's wonderfully sad, drug-dragged laughter.

Tears rose to Vida's eyes. "That's it," she said. "I need to sleep now. You come back some other night."

Locking the club doors she climbed the stairs to her apartment, stopping briefly to smile at the working girls who, in these last minutes before dawn, were out looking for one last date.

What Vida had not told Sean was that at the age of eighteen she had killed the dealer who had been supplying her mother with drugs. In the first fragile light before sunrise, on a morning much like this, she had backed the man against a brick wall and cut his throat with a razor blade held between her teeth, as a hooker friend had taught her to. After that, wanting to keep the jazz flowing, wanting to own her own club, wanting to keep Carla alive, she had gone to work for the Mafia.

Vida was now waiting for her twenty-seventh contract.

There Aren't Any Safe Places

THEY HAD BEEN DRIVING FOR seven hours, the taxi meter clicking steadily as a metronome. Gorodish napped in the backseat while Alba, who was sitting up front next to quasi-Marley, was beginning to understand how reggae could get under one's skin.

"What kinda crib you looking for?"

"Something near the ocean, with jasmine and lots of bougainvillaea, thirty-foot ceilings, a heart-shaped swimming pool . . ."

"You be a swimming pool, mama, I'd take me a little dip before breakfast each morning."

". . . a Steinway piano for my friend back there, thirteen palm trees, jungly stuff climbing up the walls, man-eating plants that'll come and get you when you're asleep. . . ."

"You got to build a house like that, take you near six weeks."

"If nobody goes out on strike."

"See that nightclub? Friend of mine was coming out of there with his girlfriend, got shot by the cops."

"Americans do everything in Cinemascope."

"See that movie over there?"

"Nice neon."

"Another buddy of mine went there to see *Vertigo*, got himself wasted. See that supermarket? Only place in the neighborhood still does a cash business, gets held up about three times a week: perfect place, you want to get yourself killed."

"How about that motel over there?"

"That's an old story. Must be two months ago, woman got herself all cut up."

"Can you find us a quiet place by the ocean?"

"All you gotta do is ask."

Pyramid 1

ALTHOUGH IN BUSINESS only a short time, Horace Perceval III had already netted well over three million dollars. The glass pyramid in which he lived was one of six standing in the center of a thick forest of eucalyptus trees that covered part of a vast estate in Bel-Air.

Horace Perceval III was short and wore his hair

slicked back. He owned two hundred Hawaiian shirts, ten pairs of painters' pants of the same, implacable shade of cream, and three pairs, in every color made, of one particular style of shoe. Several jackets, purchased at an army-navy store, hung in his closet and were reserved for dress occasions. He also owned a raincoat. In short: a simple wardrobe.

Besides work the only thing Horace Perceval III loved was the more exotic cuisines. His address book contained the names of more than twenty chefs who came regularly to his home to prepare Cuban, Senegalese, Laotian, Brazilian, etc., meals.

Horace Perceval III rarely went out at night and that is how he had become a millionaire, for it takes a mere second's inattention for an opportunity to slip away. Even when strolling the estate grounds he carried a Cobra cordless telephone and if by chance he ventured from the house it was in a leased, computer-equipped limousine, so that he could remain in touch with his data and communications center.

His three secretaries worked eight-hour shifts; actually, they were less secretaries than personal assistants, for not only were they adept at the computer console they were also extremely intelligent, with a well-developed business sense and IQs higher than anyone else in their profession. As their salaries were figured on a percentage basis, each took home between three and five thousand dollars a week. At those prices a girl doesn't have to play dumb.

Horace Perceval III's house, a masterpiece of purity of line, had been designed by that genius, that most copied of postwar American architects, Marlowe Wrightson who, having displayed an obsession with the pyramid at the beginning of his career, was known to all as "Pharaoh."

Breathing deeply of the odor of eucalyptus, Horace Perceval III went back into his pyramid. It was six in the morning, time for his first cup of coffee and jogging session. Horace Perceval thought of himself as a child of the Century of Caffeine and Coca-Cola.

A, his morning secretary, had arrived. Horace Perceval did not call her A merely to objectify her but, rather, to save time. His other secretaries were called X and Z. B, for Boss, was reserved for himself.

This morning A was looking as fresh as a raspberry, her electrifying red hair enough to melt the sternest soul. She had a mind like a laser; seated amidst her computer consoles and peripherals she resembled nothing so much as an astronaut at the controls of a rocket ship, her intimidating glare enough to render the Information Age docile.

An indescribable bond existed between Horace Perceval III and A. They were like two computers of the same make, running the same program, with the added advantage of being able to give free rein to their human emotions. During those frequent moments of complete understanding they would often smile at each other; in an interview with *Business Week* Horace Perceval III had gone so far as to describe those synchronized smiles as "orgasmic."

When a reporter from *Playboy* dared pose an indiscreet question regarding his sex life Horace Perceval III insisted he take a picture of A's smile and demanded it be published in place of the "Playmate of the Month." So persuasive was he that, indeed, A's lips did appear as requested.

Horace Perceval III had established business relationships in every region of the United States, as well as in the principal cities of Europe and Asia. His partners were chosen by computer and received generous finder's fees for whatever business they generated, although Horace Perceval III remained the only one to know who his clients were and where they were actually located. As information flowed in from the four corners of the earth, A, or one of the other secretaries, kept a record of sales and purchases. Any partner showing a drop in productivity was immediately replaced. On an average day Horace Perceval III bought and sold one hundred sixty-seven separate items. Over the last five months his company, Biz & Biz, had become a major power in the closeouts, collectibles and memorabilia industries.

Along with his state-of-the-art computer and communications center, Horace Perceval III also owned the most modern kitchen in California. With its ten refrigerated compartments properly provisioned, the kitchen's computer-controlled robot, which had been designed by Pharaoh, and built and programmed by the junior class at Cal Tech, with menus developed by the University of California

(Davis), could prepare any one of thirty-three basic dishes. Purveyors of meat, fish, fruits and vegetables were on call to deliver whatever was needed. Spices, of which Horace Perceval III was inordinately fond, were always in stock.

The pyramid also contained a sleep unit. Once inside it, Horace Perceval could hear nothing but the splashing of a waterfall which had been recorded at Kyoto, the cascade of sound meshing with his brain waves to bring on sleep and sparing him the side effects that accompany sleeping pills and tranquilizers. Horace's sleep cycle was two and a half hours, three times in every twenty-four. A, X and Z relayed each other at eight-hour intervals and were instructed to wake him only in the event of extreme emergency.

The three small glass pyramids that made up the bathing unit contained a Turkish steam room, a Japanese bath and a massage area. Each day a Japanese masseur gave Horace a Shiatsu treatment; once a week a barber came to trim his shock of hair.

The pyramid also had a living area that held nothing but three huge photorealist paintings depicting aged blue-collar workers posed nude in settings reminiscent of their former trades. The paintings were signed "Strawberry," a young artist Horace Perceval had taken under his wing.

Whenever anyone commented on the lack of chairs and couches in the living area Horace Perceval III would say, "I was not put on this earth to sit."

This executive genius, this enlightened patron of

young talent, was also supporting a composer of minimalist music in the Philip Glass mold. Yet Horace Perceval never listened to the music his money helped produce, for anything inscribed within a clearly defined time perimeter aroused a fearsome anxiety in his soul, and his analyst, another brilliant personage whose research he was financing, and who appeared to be on the brink of discovering a revolutionary new type of neurosis, had advised him to avoid anything that could not be perceived and comprehended in under five seconds.

Horace Perceval III walked into his kitchen and, with all the dexterity of a blind pianist, punched in the code for one of his favorite meals: raw tuna and pollen. At that moment A's soft, soothing voice came over the intercom: "One shirt, worn by Michael Jackson on his April third television special."

"Five thousand dollars," said the Boss, swallowing a bite of tuna.

"Should I turn it around?"

"No. Make up five thousand medallions and price them at ten dollars apiece. I'm going jogging."

"Okay, love."

Horace Perceval III always ran naked on his private sand track: his acupuncturist had convinced him of the benefits of foot massage and his Indian guru, Baba Ramesh Baba, Esq., recommended fresh air flowing over the nude body as a sort of inverted prana.

As he was passing the pyramid for the tenth time his Cobra buzzed. Horace looked over at A. In an effort to avoid an erection that would only have made the jogging more difficult, she did not return his smile.

"Bette Davis's dress and shoes from the establishing shot of Margo Channing in *All About Eve.*"

"The black dress with the brooch?"

"Yes."

"Twelve thousand. Offer it, as is, to Hso Pink Shiu, Hong Kong: thirty thousand, U.S. I'm keeping the shoes as a memento."

Putting the Cobra on standby, Horace Perceval III resumed jogging. The breeze was fragrant. Two minutes later he was interrupted again.

"Carmen Bongo's still crazy about J.R. She's willing to pay seven hundred for his Stetson, if we can get hold of it."

"Order one in a large head size and have one of the gardeners wear it for a week. You might also offer her a gold replica of the bullet that almost killed J.R.: five hundred."

Horace Perceval III slogged on around the sand track. For someone about to celebrate his tenth birthday he wasn't doing badly at all. The fact that his secretaries were all one or two years older than he, and on the far side of latency, was a minor matter, one easily handled psychotherapeutically.

She Sat Perfectly Still, Just Looking

PSEUDO-MARLEY DUMPED GORodish on the bed in Apartment 5 of the Sea Sprite Motel, a little miracle of a place on the ocean at Hermosa Beach. Alba forked over three hundred dollars and her new buddy disappeared into the night whistling "Rumba." She turned off the lights.

The apartment consisted of a kitchen, a bar, a living room, a TV set bolted to the floor, and two double beds. Gorodish was sleeping like someone recovering from a suicide attempt; there was no way Alba could rouse him sufficiently to appreciate the beauty and magic of the place. From the bay window she could see a sky-blue lifeguard tower, a dimly lit pier and phosphorescent foam atop black ocean waves. The view reminded her of dreams she had had as a child. Outside, on the sand, two black men drunkenly rode a seesaw.

The light in the sky wavered. Alba slid open the balcony door and leaned over the railing. Downstairs, a man was filling the newspaper vending machine. Iodine air whipped her face and body. Powerful waves rolled in and broke on the sand, chasing tiny birds before them.

A green cape appeared to her left. Six factory

chimneys stood silhouetted against the sky. Alba went down to the beach, sat perfectly still and let her senses run riot.

Pyramid 2

ANOTHER GLASS PYRAMID served as Strawberry's studio. At the age of seven she had developed a passion for art, in the beginning painting lyrical abstractions heavily influenced by the works of de Kooning. Later, as she grew older, a hunger for reality had overcome her; not the air-brush reality of the American photorealists but something more substantial, quivering with life, closer in spirit to the works of an Edward Hopper.

To develop her eye and hand Strawberry had begun by painting a series of empty rooms and service stations, and had attended classes taught by an academic painter of no significant talent. Then, one day, while visiting a building site, she had seen a naked construction worker come out of a tool shed and bathe himself in the water flowing from a broken overhead pipe. The sight of the water streaming down that well-muscled body had fascinated her, had stimulated her, artistically, almost as much as had the Hopper exhibit she had seen in Chicago.

Strawberry gave the sixteen-year-old Mexican construction worker her studio address and offered him ten dollars an hour to pose for her wearing nothing but his yellow hard hat. Chico, for that was his name, stared at her in delight and offered to pose for free: one rarely saw girls like Strawberry anywhere except in the movies.

Strawberry's black hair was cropped short. Her eyes seemed to devour her face and Chico took the dark circles around them as an indication of an active sex life when actually they were the mark of long hours spent before an easel.

After the first experience with Chico, for whom she had definitely felt a sexual attraction, Strawberry came to the conclusion that it would be a far more productive division of labor to hire retired blue-collar workers as her models and have sex with teenagers. She also raised her modeling fee to twenty dollars an hour. To date she had painted sixty-four life-sized nudes.

Strawberry's pyramid stood some six hundred feet from the one in which her adored, and sole, financial backer, Horace Perceval III lived. Compared to the other buildings in Pyramid City, it was simple, its interior furnished with gigantic easels, most of which were turned to the wall, a king-size waterbed and a platform where her worn-out models posed. There was also a rolling bookcase crammed with several hundred art books, and an eclectic collection of records and tapes.

When working, Strawberry often listened to a

recording made for her by Pearl O'Pearl, Pyramid City's composer-in-residence, a reading of Leonardo da Vinci's *Treatise on Painting* in the original Italian, with background sound provided by a looped tape of pygmies singing.

Since Strawberry detested the flat look of acrylic paints, the pyramid was redolent of linseed oil and turpentine.

Thanks to Horace Perceval's financial and emotional support Strawberry knew that one day her paintings would hang in the world's greatest museums. Horace had also promised that when she finished her seventieth canvas he would throw a party and ensure her success in the art world by inviting the most influential critics, gallery owners and museum directors. But for now he was adamant that nobody see her work.

A fifteen-ton, red tractor-trailer gave a blast of its horn and Strawberry watched as its incredible chrome radiator and twin overhead exhausts crept across an irremediably blue sky.

She began squeezing tubes of color onto the glass square that served as her palette.

Tony, a truck driver with biceps that would have made a weight lifter pale with envy, was her latest model. He was seventy-two, his skin as wrinkled as a dried apple and gaudy with copies of Matisse nudes tattooed on him by a French artist. It was that divine distortion, those muscles now as moth-eaten as the works of Proust, that had stirred an almost De Quinceyian ecstasy in Strawberry's soul.

So much so that she had even fronted the money for the truck rental, which turned out to be far more expensive than her human model. Luckily, Horace Perceval III had allocated funds for the emergency.

"Hey, there, Bitty Berry," said Tony, dragging himself from the cab.

"Hiya, Pops," said Strawberry, who, now that she was twelve, occasionally rose to heights of eloquence.

"This here's the exact same truck I used to drive," said Tony. "Used to be I could watch the road and feel up them hitchhiking dollies at the same time. Those were the days, girl: flower power, coast-to-coast speed spansules, everyone fuckin anythin that moved."

"What a beautiful concept," said Strawberry. "Why don't you climb back into your truck while I set up my paints and canvas? It's too bad old age withers and custom stales one's prowess in that area."

"Hey, no way, Bitty Berry. You shuck your clothes, I bet I could maybe still manage it."

"The main problem would be in holding the pose," said Strawberry. "Perhaps I could snap a Polaroid of your erection."

"Whatever."

"Good. I'll strip, too. But you must promise me not to pump up your biceps. I want them in their usual flabby state. And leave the truck door open. Through Matisse I shall pay an indirect homage to the pearly sexual organs seen in paintings by the great Shunga masters."

I Don't Make the Kind of Music You Like to Hear

THE GUN MADE SUCH SOFT music it could barely be heard. Loud conversation, or a radio playing, was enough to cover the sound. It was not a particularly discreet weapon: twelve inches long and weighing some four and a half pounds, it resembled a black steel opium pipe to which someone had added a magazine containing six 9-mm rounds. This jewel of British engineering genius had been designed as a professional killer's tool. Invented for use in close-work assassinations, it had been adopted by several resistance and terrorist groups and, even earlier, by the OSS, whose agents had fallen in love with it. Despite its age the Welrod had seen action in Vietnam, Northern Ireland and the Falkland Islands. In the 1960s the Military Armament Corporation had developed an advanced model: it was this newest version of the Welrod that Vida used.

Her career as a Mafia killer had gone well from the first. The organization did not lack for button-men who could liquidate your small-time trouble-maker for ten or fifteen thousand dollars, but when it came to operating among the higher levels of management there were fewer applicants capable of performing the job. The fee for one of these more "delicate" murders might be in excess of one hundred thousand dollars, but Vida was long past that stage of her career and now only accepted contracts for what were considered impossible hits, the money she earned being in proportion to the risks she took.

Anyone but Vida might have been content with the exorbitant fees and relatively easy work, but she had always needed to test herself, to push beyond her own limits. This constant dicing with death was a sort of deferred suicide. Vida was aware of it; it excited her.

Vida had turned killing for hire into an art form, a high wire on which she danced without a net, seeking out danger for its own sake as if the gamble itself were the crowning achievement of her life. She also knew it was absurd to always use the same gun: ballistic forensics could easily establish the identity of a weapon, and links between her many hits were easily uncovered, but it was her way of challenging society and openly flouting its laws.

Vida felt no moral compunctions about her work. Her mission was not to reestablish some illusory sort of justice but rather to fulfill herself as an artist.

The Welrod was her instrument, death her music.

The Moon's Four Days Off the Full

WHEN THE MOON FADED TO blue Alba walked to the ocean and, fully dressed, entered the water. The swells were as strong as a tidal wave and swept her off her feet. A yellow machine was raking the sand. The driver had to pull her to safety.

"We find stiffs out here every day," he said. "You better be careful. The waves around here are something fierce, and there's a riptide."

The sand was turning warm. Alba let her clothes dry, then went to do some shopping at a small grocery store across from the pier. The market was run by a Japanese woman.

Digging a fistful of damp dollars from her pocket Alba bought things she had never seen before: "Philadelphia Cream Cheese" for Gorodish, because there was an orchestra with almost exactly the same name, whole wheat English muffins, mangoes and papayas. She also bought more familiar items, things identifiable by their anglicized names or shapes: orange juice, coffee, milk, sugar, salt and pepper. And a local newspaper. And for Gorodish, that lush, a bottle of Eno Salts.

On her way back to the motel she passed a rabbi, *payess* waving in the wind as he glided along on roller skates, a large Mexican man walking on his hands, an old woman who had to be a hundred riding a skateboard, two tall, bleached-out blonds carrying weights and running, and a *karateka* fighting off an invisible army. She also saw her first police car. Siren howling, it came skidding to a stop.

She Seemed a Bit Fragile This Morning

VIDA USUALLY MET HER EM-
ployers on Mulholland Drive, the endless, tortuously curved road that had undoubtedly been chosen for the way it snaked across the hills overlooking Los Angeles, and because the sight of a limousine was no rarity there. In some places the narrow road ran through areas filled with marvelous trees and greenery; in others, clusters of houses, each more luxurious than the next, waited for a mud slide to make them affordable.

Vida liked driving along Mulholland, liked watching as the city woke to the night, dots of light forming an ocean filled with almost imperceptible waves.

Today's meeting had been set for ten in the morning. Vida had had only five hours' sleep and was feeling fragile. Parking her Impala convertible at the foot of a dirt path, she walked a few hundred feet up Mulholland. The spring rains had carved new ravines on either side of the road. From time to time in these hills a house would suddenly begin to slide then come to a stop, its rooms strangely spread-eagled.

A Prussian blue limousine pulled up beside her, the chauffeur opened the door, and Vida sat down next to the man who was her sole contact with the syndicate. He was in his sixties and resembled any other tired businessman, the sole difference being the extreme courtesy with which he greeted her. Only absolute power could permit itself to be so gracious.

"Isn't it a beautiful morning," he said. "The air is so clear today it's hard to believe that summer's almost here."

"I always thought you were a sensitive man."

"What good is life if you can't take a few minutes to enjoy the simple pleasures?"

"None at all."

Even though the window between the driver and the backseat was closed Skip turned on the radio. "I should tell you that this is a bad one. You can refuse the contract and nobody'll hold it against you. However I, personally, would feel better if you accepted it."

"A cop?"

"You've probably heard that the Cubans and Vietnamese are fighting for control of a piece of the drug trade. We thought we'd let them kill each other off, but it would take too long and, besides, it's bad for business. We've come to a temporary understanding with the Vietnamese and, as a gesture of good will, have decided to give them the top man in the Cuban organization. He's smart, never leaves himself open. The Vietnamese have already tried three times."

"How much?"

"Given the importance of the contract, and the extremely delicate situation, we're offering one hundred thousand more than last time."

"That sounds to me like a going-away present," Vida said with a cynical smile.

"We'll understand if you turn it down...."

"I'll take it."

"Sometimes I wonder what makes you tick. You can't be doing this just for the money...."

Vida looked distracted, as if she were searching for an answer to his question. Skip studied her closely. He could sense some inexhaustible need within Vida, a need that rendered her fragile, yet resolute. He did not know the origin of that need but it moved him.

"Are you in a hurry with this one?" she asked.

"Take your time."

"Do you have a file on him?"

"The Vietnamese are very thorough. We didn't

have to add a thing." He handed Vida an envelope containing photographs, a dossier, a video cassette and half her fee.

"Videotaping them now, are you?"

"It was the Vietnamese's idea. I thought it might prove helpful, give you a clearer picture of the man."

"Don't they have a kamikaze shooter of their own?"

"These days people seem less and less willing to risk their lives," said Skip. "We live in an age where there are no more great causes, no self-sacrifice. Sad, isn't it?"

"You should have been a philosopher."

"Still using the Welrod?"

"I never let it out of my sight. If I couldn't use the Welrod I'd quit the business."

"Superstitious?"

"Just trying to stay lucky."

"Call me right after it's done."

"Are you worried about me, Skip?"

"I like you very much, Vida."

Pyramid 3

PEARL O'PEARL'S PYRAMID WAS acoustically perfect and held a diverse collection of instruments ranging from African harps to several ultrasophisticated synthesizers. She had already composed more than twenty major works, including two film scores, all of which had been recorded in her sixteen-track-equipped studio. Los Angeles being a mother lode of musicians Pearl had no problem hiring people to play her music. She had even recorded the complete, uncut version of her masterwork, *Pyramid*, sixty-two minutes, three seconds of sound considered, in the words of *The New York Times*, "an event of major importance in the world of contemporary American music."

Pearl, herself, admitted to having been influenced by both Monteverdi and the Pacific Ocean. The sounds she attempted to achieve were like a cascade of pearls gleaming within an infinite tide of vesperal murmurings. For the last three months she had not once left the pyramid and was subsisting on a diet of cereal, dried fruit and milk. This self-discipline would remain in effect until she finished *Orpheus*, which had been commissioned by the Los Angeles Philharmonic and was scheduled to premiere at the last concert of the season.

Horace Perceval III, whom Pearl had affectionately nicknamed "The Sexiest Computer in Silicon Valley," had been generous in providing her with electronic equipment. Whenever she needed some new device all Pearl had to do was walk across the garden and ask for it.

Pearl's musical vocation had been revealed to her one night on the beach at Venice. She had been ten at the time, and in the throes of a mystical crisis. When the waves spoke, Pearl solemnly accepted the dictates of the ocean as others might accept God. Repudiating Satan, who had suddenly revealed himself in the combined forms of Bill Haley and Elvis Presley, she began studying music and, in memory of that night of revelation, and as a sign of her submission to a greater power, had vowed to wear nothing but jeans and faded blue T-shirts. Jeans and T-shirts became her signature and those who knew her accepted the fact that she would never wear anything else, not even for the opening of *Orpheus*.

Since that mystical night Pearl had not cut her bronze-colored mane, claiming that the hair waving about her head served as a majestic antenna to capture cosmic waves that irrigated her brain and subtly caressed her synapses. At times her hair crackled with static electricity and she resembled a lion with almond-shaped eyes and a greedy mouth tinted deep sea blue.

For the cover of her first album an art director had created a photomontage of Pearl floating naked high above the waves, backlighting giving her hair a silvery aura. A makeup artist had painted spiral staves down her long thighs, the curving, parallel lines bearing the opening bars of the album, the dark pubic triangle a pyramid, of course, a caldron from which came a concentration of an infinite number of eighth and sixteenth notes, to draw the listener down into velvet-lined nothingness.

Petunia Doesn't Like Spaghetti

"PETUNIA DOESN'T LIKE SPA-ghetti," Gorodish said quite distinctly.

Alba drew near, a glass of Eno Salts in her hand. "What did you say?"

"I was dreaming. Why don't you go to Rue de Seine and buy some croissants?"

"We're in America. Here, drink this: it's a magic potion for grown-up gorillas."

Alba threw herself into Gorodish's arms, covered his face with kisses, then pulled him to the bay window.

"I must admit, it's better than Rambouillet," he said. "How did you find it?"

"Pseudo-Marley," said Alba, propping Gorodish against a barstool so that he faced the ocean. She forced half the glass of salts down his throat.

"One week from now I'll have a tan better than Josephine Baker," she said.

"It's paradise," croaked Gorodish.

"You see: I was right when I chose Los Angeles."

"We're going to need a car."

"The biggest we can find," said Alba. "A convertible, eighteen feet long, with a sky-blue leather interior."

"All right," said Gorodish. "Do you have any idea what you'd like to do after that?"

"I think I'll have a spiritual crisis," said Alba.

Pyramid 4

AT THE AGE OF EIGHTEEN Suzy had dropped out of Berkeley to live with the most fascinating man she had ever met. For fifteen years things had gone swimmingly; then one morning she woke up to find the pool was empty. Since it's never too late, Suzy enrolled at UCLA to take the degree in literature she had earlier abandoned for the sake of love and the revolution.

Her one problem was that the bookcases narrowed at the top of the pyramid and, in obedience to the laws of topology, the highest shelf was empty. To make up for the architect's error Suzy had inserted cardboard boxes in the empty spaces and now all her manuscripts were triangular.

Suzy's face had never lost its adolescent round-ness. Her diligence in class, and her attendance at lectures and seminars to hear prestigious writers speak, only added to her juvenile appearance. Suzy lunched at the Student Union, came home at all hours, went to dorm parties and lived a life of total freedom.

Yet, this afternoon, with the complete works of Vladimir Nabokov sitting on her desk next to the battered IBM typewriter, Suzy realized that she had only one night left in which to reread and correct her doctoral thesis: "Nabokov and The Motel." Since her faculty adviser was even crazier than the most radical of the other doctoral candidates, Suzy had chosen to break the bonds of academic convention and now happily skimmed the beginning of her dissertation:

"The attribution of credit for inventions and discoveries is often a matter of historical caprice and whimsy. Since it is commonly agreed the Chinese reached America before Columbus and his European predecessors, invented noodles well before the advent of Marco Polo, and produced paper while Western man was still struggling to perfect parchment, the linear mind might be tempted to believe they also invented The Motel. Did Lao-Tse, voyaging across China on his water buffalo, stop at the occasional motel before merging with the eternal Tao? I often ponder such questions.

"Furthermore, if paper had never been invented would writers sculpt their words in stone or would they, with nonchalant hand, trace letters in the damp sand while awaiting the next wave? Odds are that, lacking paper, the world would know nothing but masterpieces of the writer's art, but whether of sheer stubbornness and determination, or of pure literary genius, is hard to say.

"Also, since certain southeast Asian tribal groups consider a kiss on the lips the most vile of sexual practices, has our own behavior been modified by the invention of the cinema and the constant repetition, both visual and auditory, of the interminable Hollywood Kiss? The first Hollywood Kiss dates from 1896 with the appearance of a thirty-second short subject. Today the world record is one hundred thirty hours, reported to have been set in a New York City store window, although no filmed evidence of the event can be traced. Is the fact that the record is held by Americans an accident? Of course not: were not dance marathons invented by William Irish and Horace MacCoy? One must never underestimate the influence of Art on either species behavior or industrial development.

"As for The Motel: I have come to the conclusion, which I intend to prove by Socratic argument, that it was discovered in May 1941 by a member of the Russian intelligentsia freshly disembarked in New York. This eminent individual, famous primarily for his expertise regarding, and enthusiasm for, butterflies, is also known for a best-selling novel, a singular tale of repressed passion in which the main theme, Love, is expressed in adroit abstractions and which has, as its incandescent central figure, The Motel. The Russian savant is, naturally, Vladimir Nabokov, and the novel, *Lolita*."

A Flossy Cadillac

AFTER FIVE CUPS OF COFFEE brewed from Guatemala Antigua beans, Gorodish finally realized that the blue thing out there making waves was probably the ocean, the long blond stretch of stuff was sand, and Alba was still Alba. Gazing at the small breasts burgeoning delicately beneath the pink T-shirt he wondered if it was jet lag that had suddenly made them larger. It then occurred to him that Alba was striding toward her fourteenth birthday in seven-league boots. An indescribable panic took hold of him.

"Is there something wrong, dear heart?" asked Alba.

"About this spiritual crisis of yours..."

"We've got to buy a car, can't even *sneeze* around here without a car, got to get us a car. And some books."

"Books? What kind of books?"

"I don't know exactly. Books about guys who get buried alive, guys who levitate, guys who go into a trance."

"Look out the window," said Gorodish. "Some

idiots down there are shaking tambourines and ring-
ing bells."

Alba carried her glass of milk to the window and
stared down at a dozen or so shaved heads and orange
sheets.

"Looks like they've got Saint Vitus's Dance," she
said. "I can spot a phony a mile away: they're not
the real thing."

"Their guru probably rides around in a Rolls-
Royce and spends his days swilling Manhattans
beside a lotus-scented pool."

"There have to be some real ones around," said
Alba. "The part that interests me is not needing
anything to get high."

"Let's go buy a Cadillac," said Gorodish. "Now
that's *my* idea of a meditation mantra."

A half hour later a taxi dropped Gorodish and
Alba in front of a Hollywood car lot belonging to
The King of Used Cadillacs. His Majesty had done
things in a big way: every model of Cadillac manufactured since 1936 was on display, as well as a
few vintage models, and several limousines that had
seen so little service they were practically virgin.

Holding hands, Gorodish and Alba wandered up
and down the rows of gleaming cars. A syrupy-
voiced salesman, tie as garish as a Bolshoi Theater
stage set, hair gelled and shiny, greeted them: "Can
I help you folks?"

"How long would it take for me to drive one of
these beauties off the lot?" asked Gorodish.

"The time it takes to sign a check and drop by

an insurance agency. And it just so happens we can handle that for you, too."

"Which one do you want, Alba?"

"Tell Mr. Vaseline to butt out," she said. "This is a serious decision and I need time to think."

"Why don't you have your insurance coconspirator come over," Gorodish suggested. "While we're waiting for him we'll choose a car."

"It never snows here," said Alba. "We want a convertible."

"One that runs, if possible," said Gorodish, "at least long enough to drive back to the motel."

Alba had come to a stop in front of a pair of white fins decorated with protruding lights that resembled twin red bananas. "Look at that rear end."

"A 1959 Cadillac Eldorado Biarritz convertible," the salesman said in hushed tones; "78,657 miles, twelve thousand dollars."

Worshipfully, they opened the car doors. "They're heavy enough for a safe," Alba whispered.

The seats were white leather, the steering wheel resembled ivory. There was even the original, factory-installed radio. The salesman held up the keys; they jingled like bells. Gorodish looked under the hood. It wasn't a motor; it was a peach Melba. They drove around the block. Gorodish paid cash. They headed down Santa Monica Boulevard.

"You can't lose your way in Los Angeles," he said. "Every boulevard leads to the ocean."

Three hours later they found themselves in the Mojave Desert, far from water but happy.

Pyramid 5

I N THE DEPTHS OF THE VAST, shadowy grounds the pyramids gleamed like ant-arctic ice. Only the one belonging to Dr. Kim Breuerfliess, Psychoanalyst, glowed dimly behind its bamboo blinds.

At the urging of friends, and under the rigorously Freudian influence of cocaine, Dr. Breuerfliess had recently completed her doctorate. Although new to the profession, she was already known to her colleagues, primarily through the publication of several studies in a few of the more prestigious psycho-analytic journals. For the last three months Kim had been working on a theory that, if proven, would doubtless appear in all future psychology textbooks as the Breuerfliess Syndrome.

Her research centered on the long-term obser-vation of a single patient, a world-famous celebrity known for the complexity of his thought processes and whose neuroses had resisted all previous forms of therapy. Yet, during his first session with Dr. Breuerfliess, her perspicacity and intuition had evoked an immediate response in him; after that she had slowly begun building the theoretical arma-ture on which to hang the blockbuster conclusions she was now planning to present at the next Psychoanalytic Association conference in Osaka.

Until now Kim had kept those conclusions to herself, but tonight, as she put the final touches on her article, she suddenly decided to share them with her patient. After which she would certainly have to go thank Horace Perceval III, without whose generosity she would never have been able to pursue her research.

In her very best hand, Kim wrote:

Pyramid 5, Twilight

Dearest Tut-Tut,
    Pardon me for troubling the silence of your retreat but the great day is here, and I'm ready to tell you the conclusions I have reached. Do come as quickly as you can, and don't forget to bring my nose candy. A new life is about to begin for you. Osaka will be my Iwo Jima.

Your loving,
Kim Kong

At this hour of the evening the pyramid was filled with honey-colored light. Kim stripped off her clothes and lay down on her psychoanalyst's couch, an air mattress floating in a round pool set in the center of the pyramid. The mattress was under-inflated just enough so that it would sink slightly beneath a patient's weight, lowering him partway into the body-temperature water. Kim found that the gentle bobbing of the air mattress served to rid her patients of their inhibitions; occasionally it also aroused in them a sudden passion for canoeing.

Since her favorite patient never saw anyone before eleven at night, Kim waited. Later, wet and naked, breathing deeply of the odor of eucalyptus, she went out into the garden and walked through the deep grass toward the pigeon coop. Placing the message, which was written on a small square of paper, in a holder strapped to a carrier-pigeon's leg, Kim launched the bird into the night. Then, laughing, she headed back toward her pyramid, stopping halfway to shout into the darkness: "Charcot! Freud! Jung! Lucan! Breuerfliess!"

Of Course You Are Crazy

MARLOWE WRIGHTSON, who, in their intimate moments, Dr. Breuerfliess called Tut-Tut, and whose birth certificate read Jeremy David (a name confirmed when a hard-shell Baptist minister plunged him, full immersion, into the Arkansas River), was known to the rest of the world as Pharaoh.

At the age of sixteen Pharaoh had discovered architecture and the works of Raymond Chandler, and never looked back. Entering Berkeley, he managed to combine the two prime passions of his life (not counting politics) in the writing of an honors program dissertation on Chandlerian architecture, a good portion of which was based on a field study during which he spent several months photographing buildings evocative of Chandler's universe. He was particularly proud of having uncovered several houses that appeared to have been built according to descriptions in his favorite author's novels, his greatest discovery being a replica of Terry Lenox's home, in Encino. Today, those same photographs hung on the walls of his studio and were the sole images, outside his own architectural designs, that he could abide.

It seemed quite natural when his fellow students began calling him Marlowe but it had taken some doing, several years of a single-minded passion for straight lines, for him to become "Pharaoh." Now, at the age of forty-seven, he had reached the pinnacle of his profession. His genius, his way of life, his personal habits, his refusal to take the usual pathway to success, had done as much for his reputation as had his buildings and complexes.

To the public, Pharaoh appeared an impassioned and solitary figure; while most of his colleagues and competitors headed large architectural firms he continued working alone, with no secretary or assistant to aid him.

Work began each morning at five. At two

Pharaoh lunched at the Grand Central Market, nearby, in the heart of downtown Los Angeles. Later, after a two-hour stroll, he returned to his studio to answer his mail, writing in a bold hand, the words sprawling across the gray paper.

His studio took up the entire top floor of a building that dated back to the 1930s. The huge room with its worn floor was painted a light, restful gray, the pale walls serving as dramatic backdrop to the display of Pharaoh's black-and-white photographs. The room held two large tables lit by draftsman's lamps. There was also a Mexican hammock where he often napped before returning to his drafting table to work, often until midnight.

One corner of the studio was reserved for models and maquettes. Pharaoh preferred building the mockups of his projects himself, finding the manual labor that went into making the models of enormous help in visualizing his ideas.

Rice paper covered the studio windows, filtering the light and filling the room with a soft, steady glow. No one was ever allowed to visit the studio. There was no telephone. Pharaoh never listened to music while he worked; the only sound was the whisper of the air-conditioner.

He worked standing, his tall, thin body crouching over the table, moving silently, barefoot, one hand pushing back his long hair, a pencil in the other tracing the delicate lines that, even in their earliest stage, seemed more art than technology.

Pharaoh had such a passion for detail that he took

on only those projects in which he could also design the interiors and furniture. His work had appeared in every encyclopedia of architecture published in the last twenty years, and on his last visit to Hennessy and Ingalls, the Wilshire Boulevard shop specializing in books on architecture, he had found nine monographs relating to his work. Not a day passed that some young architect did not ask to study with him. Each summer Pharaoh spent one month teaching and had already signed contracts that for the next twelve years would take him to every major school of architecture in the world.

At present Pharaoh was working on the plans for a concert hall in Singapore. He had already decided that it would have no seats; instead, the space would be filled with wavelike elements, the stage their focal point and the trough of each wave furnished with rugs and cushions on which the audience would recline, in Pharaoh's opinion the optimal posture for listening to music. In order to give his imaginary ocean an added touch of extravagance, Pharaoh had written to China and ordered two thousand eight hundred copies of a nineteenth-century Pao-tou carpet in midnight blue with turquoise motifs and brilliant red and yellow lozenges and flowers.

Among Pharaoh's more famous buildings was a California home in which one entire wall was a transparent swimming pool. One entered the water from the roof. Rooms built on elevators moved up and down, according to the view, or light, desired. From one side the swimmers looked out over the ocean, from the other, into twenty-five feet of blue water.

His first major project, for a Persian Gulf emir, had attracted worldwide attention. Hired to build a desert palace, he had cunningly designed it in the form of dunes whose sandy sinuosities so merged with the surrounding environment as to render them almost invisible.

His most ambitious project had been canceled by the City of New York due to a lack of funds and the difficulties inherent in its design. In an attempt to ease traffic in Manhattan, Pharaoh had envisioned building a bridge the entire length of the island and constructing replicas of the city's most beautiful skyscrapers upside down beneath it, positioning them not only to reflect the existing buildings but also to serve as supports for the entire structure. The new skyscrapers would not only have been habitable they would also have been linked to their counterparts so that the public might cross over, or under. In either case the people of New York would have had an extraordinary view of their city.

Undismayed by the setback, and fascinated by the idea of duplicating midtown Manhattan in negative space, Pharaoh continued to work on the project, refining its details and dreaming of the day it would be a reality.

The sole means of communication Pharaoh could bear was carrier pigeon. Now he heard scratching, and the sound of a beak pecking. Opening the message, he read Dr. Breuerfliess's invitation and decided to accept.

Taking his Renault Alliance from the underground parking lot, Pharaoh made a short stop at Main Street to find his favorite dealer, then, half an hour later, entered the peace and quiet of another of his masterpieces, Pyramid City.

The day's work had gone well. Pharaoh was in a good mood. He therefore decided to visit each of the pyramids before having to face Dr. Breuerfliess and her theory.

Such a Sad, Beautiful Name

THE RED-AND-GREEN NEON sign in the window flashed PALM READING, TAROT, LUCK. Beyond the window was a small living room hung with curtains which were drawn whenever a client was having her fortune told. Tristana was about to turn off the sign when she noticed Vida's Chevy Impala.

She opened the door and the two women embraced. "I haven't seen you in, how long is it, three months? Things must be going right for you, like I predicted."

"I don't want to talk about the past," said Vida. She held out a bouquet of yellow tulips, Tristana's favorite flower.

"You shouldn't have," said Tristana, searching for a vase. The small kitchen was papered with postcards from satisfied customers, the cards forming a varied and colorful landscape of ocean views and mountain vistas.

"A glass of port?"

"Don't mind if I do."

They sat on the couch. Tristana took Vida's hand and caressed it with her wrinkled brown fingers.

"The usual?"

"Yes. I need to know if next Friday is a lucky day for me."

Tristana fell silent and closed her eyes. After a few minutes sweat appeared on her forehead. At last she opened her eyes.

"Yes. You will succeed in all you undertake. Did you want to ask me a question about love?"

"You mean there are people who still believe in it?"

"Yes. My clients."

She Smiled
at Me Vaguely

ALBA HAD NOT BEEN HER-self since the day she had loaded the Cadillac's trunk with books. She had taken to rising with the sun, beginning each morning with a long, solitary walk on the beach, breathing deeply as she waded through the lazy fading waves. She could feel "things happening inside," a phrase she always used when trying to describe her sudden transformation.

After her morning walk she sat down on the sand, faced the ocean and read her damn books until around nine when she returned to the motel and prepared a meal of milk and fruit such as bananas or mangoes. This was not precisely the breakfast Gorodish was hoping for: he needed a good cup of coffee and a half-dozen croissants to get him started.

It was not that he was against Alba immersing herself in another culture; it was merely that he worried his angel might find herself caught up in some philosophical chop-suey invented by one of the California gurus. From time to time, just to keep an eye on things, he would peek into her books; luckily, they all seemed serious enough. The problem was that the situation had become both simple

and complicated. Naturally, it amused him to watch
Alba float through that labyrinth of Orientalia with
all the ease of a Siren splashing her way up the
Danube. And it wasn't as if there was anything
specific to complain about, exactly; it was just that
Alba had become vague and distracted, moving
through the days with a small smile on her lips,
speaking rarely, uninterested in shopping sprees,
going out at night, movies or eating in fine restaurants. The motel room seemed to be enough for her
and she appeared to have settled into a steady diet
of cream cheese, English muffins and tomatoes.

After breakfast Alba would play in the water,
hopping up and down in the surf like a little girl,
before returning to the motel room to read. At
night, when the beach was deserted, she would go
out again and run a mile or two in her bare feet;
when she came back her skin tasted of salt. If Gorodish kissed her she displayed neither enthusiasm nor
distaste and he was beginning to feel that she was
slowly changing into a bronze Buddha, one to whom
he was expected to build a temple, make daily offer-
ings of flowers and address prayers. Gorodish was
not completely materialistic, nor was he a hide-
bound atheist; his was an accommodating nature,
but Alba's recent behavior was driving him nuts.

There finally came a day when she walked in
carrying the complete works of Chuang-tsu, sat down
at the table and began to sieve bananas and mangoes
through her teeth. Primed with three cups of coffee,
Gorodish decided it was time for a talk with his

angel, whose skin was turning a miraculous shade of copper, and whose hair was blonder than ever. He leaned back against the bar.

"Did you sleep well?"

"Wonderfully," said Alba.

"Interesting book?"

"Want to read it?"

"I was asking your opinion."

"A personal opinion can never be more than a partial view of a subject," said Alba.

"Is that what your whaChuangmacallit says?"

"You seem worried."

"I *would* be happier if you talked to me more often."

"An absence of words leads to the silence of the spirit."

"I'd rather listen to music," said Gorodish, draping one arm over Alba's shoulder and caressing her forehead, her face. She closed her eyes.

"That's more like it," Gorodish said softly, and kissed her.

"I have yet to experience the sudden interior illumination," said Alba. "I am as yet unlearned, but one day it will all come together and I will be one with the Tao."

"And I shall be your first disciple," said Gorodish. "I could turn it into a nice little moneymaking proposition, build you a white temple in Palos Verdes. . . ."

Alba laughed a delicious little morning laugh. Gorodish's stomach unclenched.

"What made you choose the Tao rather than some other ism?"

"I don't know, just a feeling. There's something about all those best-seller gurus . . . I didn't want to give them my money. As for Zen, well, it's probably all right but there's too many assholes who've taken it up. And as far as the modernists go, your Castañedummies and your Gurdjishmucks, I was beginning to get confused. Then I saw this guy who looked okay, I mean, okay for someone traveling on the road to enlightenment; so I walked over and asked him a question."

"A question?"

"I said, 'Somewhere in all this shit there has to be *something* that was written before the Industrial Revolution.' He just smiled, pulled out a book of writings by the Immortals and said, 'Dig this, baby; it's aces. Nothing later than the fourth century, C.E.'"

Gorodish thoughtfully chewed one last croissant, his eyes fixed on the horizon.

"You see," Alba said very seriously, "their number is based on the idea that the Tao is unnameable, that there is no Creator, that all things spring from Nothingness. The 'Wuwei,' the superior man, practices in-action by allowing things to happen. He is primitive, simple, unambitious, undeformed by civilization. He acts according to his own nature and not that of others. Everything exists within us. Are you following this?" said Alba as she finished her milk.

Gorodish loved watching that white-rimmed mouth as it explained the essence of Taoism.

"Everything is One, there are no opposites, everything is in accord. It is man's mind alone that causes disorder, that creates true and false. The superior man has emotions but is not ruled by them. He merges with the Tao."

"Fine," said Gorodish. "You go merge; I have to work on the Cadillac: there's something wrong with the ignition."

Beautiful, ethereal, Alba smiled at him.

Hands black, body curved over the engine, Gorodish pondered the emptiness, the slow panic overtaking him. Alba was as comfortable as a tropical fish in warm water but he was having a hard time adjusting. Was he a victim of that recently discovered form of depression known as "geographic displacement"?

In an attempt to define his malaise Gorodish decided to draw up a list of the differences that might be affecting him:

The croissants tasted different;
In restaurants, the servings of food covered the plates from rim to rim;
California wines tasted of the raw grape;
The women were too tan, too muscular, too healthy, too well coiffed, too liberated. Roller skating, skateboarding, bicycling they moved too quickly for the eye to appreciate them;
American attitudes regarding personal hygiene were too sophisticated: deodorants were ruining his sense of smell;

In Italian restaurants the pasta was cooked too long;

Californians were addicted to white wine;

American beef was not Charolais, American chickens did not come from Bresse, and even aspirin tasted different;

There were too many commercials on television;

American cars were too comfortable;

American beds were too big, and the pillows were rectangular;

Instead of being included in the menu, daily "specials" were recited by the waiters and he could never remember them;

"Classic" buildings were thirty years old;

He was homesick;

He was jealous of the good-looking young men on the beach;

He was afraid of the competition;

Making love had been turned into a sport;

Alba was too beautiful, too desirable, too free, too intelligent, too mystical, too tan, too vegetarian, too philosophical;

He had no desire to buy a bicycle or sign up at a health club;

Every concert listed in the newspaper was too far away;

The city was too big;

He usually missed his freeway exit, or found himself in the lane marked RIGHT LANE MUST EXIT;

Pastrami was too good;

The coleslaw was too sweet;

The Statue of Liberty was French;

He could feel himself sinking into quicksand, a frog too old to make it to the next lily pad.

In Hollywood
Anything Can
Happen, Anything
at All

HORACE PERCEVAL III SAT counting the profits from his last twelve hours' work. Although the youngest in the family, in some respects Horace was its pillar of strength. Hearing his father's voice, he looked up.

"How's business?" asked Pharaoh.

"Just fine. We've grossed twenty-eight percent more than last month and it's starting to look like we're going to have our best quarter yet. The only problem is my partners; they all seem to lose their talent for business when they reach fifteen or sixteen. I watch them fade into a fog of puberty and wonder if I'll wind up that way, too."

"Don't worry," said Pharaoh. "Even if you lose ninety percent of your business sense there will be enough money for you to retire; you'll never wind up on the street."

"I'm determined to keep up my philanthropic work," said Horace. "That reminds me, during a slight lull in trading this afternoon I worked out a way for you to better your cash flow by four hundred twenty-seven percent. Now if you'll only listen to me and . . ."

In spite of himself, Pharaoh smiled: Horace Perceval was always teasing him about his inability to turn his reputation into money.

"Do you have some raw tuna and pollen?" asked Pharaoh.

They ate standing up in the kitchen. "One of these days I'll give a dinner party and serve nothing but African food," said Horace. "I think I'll invite the governor. He's approached me about going on public television to give a course based on my theories regarding prepubescent entrepreneurs. Will you come?"

"I shall be happy to, Horace. And I thank you for the Chandler novel: I appreciate the thought."

"You look tired. Maybe you need to get more sleep."

"My creativity seems to be at its highest around dawn."

The Cobra buzzed. Pharaoh left his son and walked to the next pyramid where his daughter, Strawberry, was working on a canvas. Deeply satisfied, he stood and watched her for a long moment.

"How do you like Tony?" asked Strawberry. She was wearing a very flattering kimono made of peach silk.

"First rate, first rate; in good shape for his age."

"He does give one reason to hope, doesn't he?"

"I stopped on Main Street to buy some coke," said Pharaoh, "and thought you might like a little grass." He handed her a plastic packet containing two ounces of the finest Hawaiian weed.

"How sweet," said Strawberry. "You do think of everything, don't you? One of these days I'll have to preserve you for posterity by painting your portrait."

"You seem to be worried about something," said Pharaoh.

"I'm pregnant again."

"Tony?"

"No, the young Mexican model before him."

"Let me know when you go for the abortion and I'll come to the clinic with you. And don't hesitate to ask if you need money. I hope you don't mind my saying this but you really ought to start taking the contraceptive pill, or choose men who've had a vasectomy."

"You know I don't like anything that isn't absolutely natural, Papa."

"I hope you'll forgive me for being so blunt. . . ."

"Not at all. You're wonderful. And it's lovely of you to want to go to the clinic with me, but I think I'm going to keep this one."

"I *am* glad," said Pharaoh, and kissed his daughter.

"If it's a boy I'll call him Pharaoh, and if it's a girl, Pyramid."

"You can't know how happy you've made me. Now, you take care of yourself. Don't work too hard, and let me know how you're getting on."

Pharaoh felt as if he were soaring: the idea of becoming a grandparent, and that his grandchild might be named after him, filled him with joy. He floated to a stop in front of the pyramid belonging to Pearl who, at sixteen, was his oldest child. Entering the acoustic pyramid he found her seated at her worktable wearing nothing but the blue tint on her eyes and lips. She stood to kiss her father; he felt strangely disturbed by her beauty.

"How is *Orpheus* coming, my darling?"

"Slowly. What about you? How is your auditorium?"

"There's one new detail . . . I'd like to make your music part of the building. We could have them play one of your works at the opening concert. That would be . . ."

"Marvelous. . . ."

"I've brought you some opium."

"I've been trying to smoke less lately. I don't want my *Orpheus* to sound completely stoned."

"You're so lovely, so tropical, so Ellingtonian. Seeing you like this has given me an idea: if you don't mind, I'd like to make a plaster cast of your body and build a house-sized version of it for an Italian client. He's purchased a magnificent site near Naples and is sending his plane for me. I'll fly over and spend a few hours with him. If you like you may accompany me. We can do the round trip in one day."

"I'd love to see Vesuvius."

"I imagine it might be absolutely splendid to live in your belly, your breasts, your mouth, your gaze."

"And it wouldn't make a bad cover for my next album, either."

Pharaoh glanced over toward Suzy's pyramid where the lights were still burning. "Your mother's been studying much too hard," he said. "I'm worried. I do hope she passes her exams."

"I would have liked to have known you when you were teaching at Berkeley," said Pearl. "I bet you seduced every girl in your class. I've also heard it said that you were something of a revolutionary. . . ."

"Oh, I've blown up a few ugly buildings in my day."

"Tell Mama to come smoke some opium with me whenever she has the time. It will help her relax."

Suzy was asleep at her desk. As he did each evening, Pharaoh read the pages scattered around the typewriter, then, using a perfectly sharpened pencil, wrote: "Audacious. Brilliant. Marvelous. But you're working too hard, my darling. Pearl asks you to come over and smoke a pipe or two with her. I think you should make time for it."

Pharaoh carried Suzy to her bed, pulled the covers up, then silently left the room. As he crossed the few yards that separated the pyramid belonging to his first wife, Suzy, from the one belonging to Kim, his second wife and Suzy's occasional lover, Pharaoh meditated on the fact that although few men managed to attain harmony in their lives he, himself, was swimming in it.

Taking off his clothes, Pharaoh joined Kim on the floating mattress. She woke and kissed him tenderly, holding his head against her breast as she caressed his forehead. Softly, she said: "You have an important decision to make. If you keep going the way you have, your neurosis will only grow worse and may even lead to a nervous breakdown. You suffer from a very rare disorder, one I've never run across in any of my other patients; in fact, it's so rare there is no mention of it in any of the literature. Your problem is that you are never under stress. You live in absolute harmony with your surroundings. Our son is a genius, as are Suzy's daughters. Your wives adore you, so there is never any conflict or hostility in your life. You are unarguably the most famous architect in the world, you work only at what pleases you with no assistant or secretary to provide the tension you need. The fact that you are having difficulty in swallowing and your other psychogenically based problems are further proof that Man is not meant to live without conflict. If you don't do something, what are now merely bothersome symptoms may become aggravated and might even lead to a loss of creativity. You are suffering from The Breuerfliess Syndrome. In fact you are the first case ever recorded."

"What sort of therapy do you suggest?" asked Pharaoh, once again amused by Kim's perspicacity.

"You must leave your harmonious world and start living in a manner more in keeping with your innermost needs."

"But what about you, and my work?"

"We don't need a man who is unfulfilled, a man who is not doing his best work. I'm afraid that you're heading for trouble, or soon will be. Your condition may very quickly grow worse. I make this suggestion as much for you as for your work: you must change your way of life."

"I have contracts to fulfill."

"You are a genius, Tut. People expect a genius to retire from public life every once in a while, to take time out from work for renewal and inspiration. You'll come back stronger and spiritually enriched."

Pharaoh let himself slip into the warm water. "Do you actually think that Providence will actually find a way to provide me with the stress I am lacking?"

"I hope so. In any case you must try."

"I don't know what I'd do with myself if I didn't have my work, and my nights with you."

"Reread Raymond Chandler."

"I don't want to have to explain about my disappearance."

"You don't have to explain a thing. Let it remain our secret."

"So I disappear, just like that, without leaving a trace, a message . . ."

"It would be simpler."

"How long shall I stay away?"

"One can never predict exactly how long a particular therapy may take. The first sign that the treatment is working will be when your physical symptoms disappear. After that you should begin to feel renewed, strengthened, filled with new ideas."

"All right," said Pharaoh, "why not? It's true, I *have* been rather tired, and it might do me some good . . . but where shall I go?"

"I don't want to know where you are but if at all possible you must choose some place in diametric opposition to your principal interests. For example, I don't think that a trip to Egypt would do. Be contrary: each time you feel an impulse, do the exact opposite."

"Our son has just given me a first edition of *The Long Goodbye*. It's the one thing I'd want to take with me."

"Fine. You might even use it as a starting point. Why not live the life of a Chandler character?"

"My clients will be in a panic, they'll search for me everywhere. They'll bother you. . . ."

"Don't worry: I'll handle everything."

"This is wonderful! I feel as if a great weight has been lifted . . ."

"See?"

"But what about the children?"

"Geniuses understand each other. I doubt they'll even ask, and I certainly won't volunteer anything. . . ."

"Then I shall leave. Would you like to . . ."

"Yes, I would. Lately you've been making love to us much less frequently. I know that Suzy has been having an affair with a student . . ."

"I'm so glad. She works much too hard."

". . . but I haven't had the time. My research . . ."

"Promise me that while I'm away . . . well, it would please me if I knew that you . . ."

"Of course. If I find a man who measures up."

Pharaoh and Dr. Breuerfliess made love until dawn. After napping awhile, he went to his own pyramid, put on an old pair of jeans, tennis shoes and a khaki vest, took fifty thousand dollars in cash, enough to last him a month or two, and left Pyramid City on foot.

On an impulse he decided to walk all the way out Sunset Boulevard to Santa Monica, arriving there, somewhat winded, three hours later.

Sitting down on a bench Pharaoh watched the white waves roll in. After a while he felt intoxicated and could sense himself being drained of all emotion. Curiously, he felt well.

He began to think of all the houses he had so patiently photographed and, remembering the one that resembled Terry Lenox's place, wondered if it still existed. His Chandlerian escapade was beginning to take shape.

You Can Kiss Me if You Like

GORODISH SPENT ALMOST AS many hours under the hood of the Cadillac as Alba did trying to merge with the Tao. They both seemed to be having a problem attaining their goal: gaining wisdom was proving to be as difficult a process as making a soufflé, while automobile repair was a complicated matter, rather as if one had placed nails in the bottom of the aforementioned soufflé dish in hopes that they would rise to the top.

When the car was running, Gorodish conscientiously drove the freeways, concentrating on the road with almost calligraphic care. But when, even with the most gentle persuasion, the *grande crème*, as Alba called it, refused to move he would take off on foot, walking all the way from Long Beach to Malibu, watching the weirdos on their roller skates, scooters, bicycles, sail skates, tricycles and sedan chairs. The natives had a lot of imagination. As he walked, Gorodish pondered his situation: he had already tried long drives and surf fishing; all that remained to him now was depression, and he could already feel that great gray glove coming dangerously near, near enough to gain a stranglehold on his brain. He was having trouble sleeping, his dreams filled with diverse beasties who insisted on dropping by for a chat. And he was losing his natural élan, his curiosity about things. For her part, Alba was sticking stubbornly to her Tao. Their breakfast conversation had begun to sound like the dialogues of Confucius and Lao-tan.

It would all have been bearable if only Gorodish were attracted to those wrinkled old Sons of Han but, to tell the truth, he would by far have preferred sipping a glass of white wine with Beethoven, or matching sixteenth notes with old Papa Bach. The one thing that might have helped was a Steinway; or a Baldwin, if worse came to worse.

Staring at the water was making him dizzy and conjured up far too many Chinese images. Gorodish turned away from the ocean and looked back at the buildings. Wood or brick, garage or warehouse, they seemed to comfort him, especially those built in the shape of a grand piano. After all, a piano doesn't guzzle gas. The bench may be hard, and the wind doesn't whistle in your ears, but no one has ever died in a piano accident, except for those musicians who get killed by the critics.

It was clear to him now that Alba would reach June 2 before she did Nirvana. She had already pushed their beds closer together, much to the joy of the Chicana chambermaids who no longer even bothered to hide their curiosity about Humberty old Gorodish and his *chulita*.

But their moments of tender intimacy had lost

much of their salt since the Chinese had come into their lives. Alba was acting as if she were trying to rebuild the Great Wall all by herself, undaunted by the enormity of the task but, then, you know how those people are: infinitely patient. There might even come a time, perhaps on the night of June 2, when Gorodish would find himself in Outer Mongolia while his nymph was still traipsing around Shanghai: he had never foreseen that possibility. In an attempt to discourage all those little people in Mao suits who were trotting around with baskets of dirt on their heads, he decided to plant a magic mountain of his own smack in the middle of their territory.

That afternoon Gorodish visited twenty-three houses ranging in style from Walt-Disno-Victorian, to neo-Frank-Lloyd-Wrong, to Viennese Pastry, to California Cantilever, to Ocean-Liner-Brick-Deco. There was even one beauty shaped like a Coco-Cola bottle on whose walls a compulsive graffiti artist had sprayed:

TAKE THE PEPSI CHALLENGE

If there was one thing in which Gorodish did believe it was luck. So, naturally, toward nightfall, it (luck) tapped him vigorously on the shoulder. Somewhere between Manhattan Beach (two fine restaurants) and Hermosa Beach (no restaurants worth the trip) he came upon a building with eaves that

seemed to be smiling to the four points of the com-
pass and roof tiles the color of jade. The house was
surrounded by small flags that floated in the wind,
while a cement menagerie that might have been
invented by the sons of the Middle Kingdom stood
guard. No doubt about it: a pagoda. Nailed to the
door facing the ocean was a red FOR SALE sign.

Gorodish rang the bell. Nothing. He kicked the
door and after a while a frightened adolescent with
a shaved head opened it.

"The Master is not receiving today. This is the
Hour of Meditation."

Gorodish pushed past him. The punky-monky
scrambled after him like a frightened chicken.

"Go tell your Master that Confucius is here and
wants to do business."

The funky-monky disappeared. Gorodish peeked
into a large room and saw what appeared to be a
choir of senior citizens trying to read a phone book.
Silence fell. The Hour of Meditation raced to a close
and most of the skinheads withdrew, like worms in
a blue cheese.

The Master, who was sitting in the lotus position
on a red pedestal, was about as Chinese as a Swissair
jet. In fact he had exactly the same accent as Gorodish's Zurich banker.

"Ave, Caesar," said Gorodish to open the bidding.

"My name is Tsu Fu. I am the sixty-fourth link
in a chain..."

"...link fence," Gorodish interrupted him. "You

look like a blintz trying to pretend it's an egg roll. I can smell the fondue from here, amigo. How much for the mosque?"

Tsu Fu quivered as the ethereal odor of cash tickled his nose. "Five hundred thousand dollars," he said.

"How big is this place, anyway?"

"Each floor is twelve hundred square feet."

"How much is that in *li*?"

"Pardon?"

"A Chinese unit of measure roughly equivalent to six hundred yards. Before I hand over the check, exactly why are you selling?"

"Problems mit der Polizei."

"I see," said Gorodish, his voice as friendly as a steamroller.

"Everything works, water, telefon, roof...."

"Good. Pack up your safe, have your flunky-monkies clean up the place and call the exterminator. I'll be back in an hour with a check for three hundred thousand Swiss francs. No need to let the IRS and the U.S. Immigration Service in on this."

"Good."

Gorodish make a quick tour of the pagoda. Apparently, the residents had been camping out in sleeping bags. There were two huge rooms, and many windows; even discounting the effects of meditation, the house seemed to soar above the ocean. The floor was bright, polished by the disciples' bare feet, but although the odor of incense had infiltrated itself everywhere, the place still stank. Gorodish decided to have it disinfected and repainted. The space, which contained nothing but a shower and a shabby little kitchen, seemed to be calling to him.

When he returned with the check, Tsu Fu was waiting with his lawyer. The papers were signed in 6/4 time and the Master was about to make his exit when Gorodish, who had skimmed more than a few of Alba's books, began to quote Wang Chung:

"Man's place in the universe is like that of a flea or louse beneath a robe or jacket. Whether it acts wisely or unwisely, can the flea or louse affect the movement of the heavens under the jacket? It cannot. And to suppose that Man alone can do so is to err regarding the principle of all things under heaven."

Properly amazed, the Zurichmeister departed. Gorodish watched his Mercedes disappear into the distance.

The exterminators were busy spraying. Gorodish greeted the cleaning crew and painters, handing them enough portraits of Ben Franklin to ensure that the pagoda would be immaculate by the next day. The Americans didn't seem to mind hard work: quite a change from the old country.

That night Gorodish did not need Valium. He had bought a bottle of Saint Amour and sat sipping it as he watched his blond Buddha. Beyond the deserted beach a red line separated the sky and ocean. Alba's enigmatic smile waxed and waned: she was becoming more and more beautiful.

"Did you have a nice day?" she asked.

Gorodish was daydreaming. "Nothing special," he said. "I took a walk. What about you?"

"At the moment I was about to forget that I had forgotten, I remembered. It's just awful, after all the work I've put into it."

Gorodish saw his Buddha pout, saw her eyelashes flutter. Two tears appeared. Alba slid into his arms and pressed close to him. Gorodish seemed to need cuddling more than she did.

They held each other tightly, passionately, until the sky turned dark.

That's the Difference Between Crime and Business. For Business You Gotta Have Capital.

WANTING TO GET A FEEL OF the ambience, Vida arrived at the Tropicana a little after it opened. The Welrod was resting comfortably in a red plastic beach bag. The ruffled black-and-purple dress and matching alligator pumps, provided by a friend in the wardrobe department at MGM, had cost her a bundle. In an attempt to look like an over-the-hill neurotic riddled with the dramatic intensity and anxiety one associates with amateur tango dancers, she had trowled on the makeup.

Catching sight of herself in a mirror Vida suddenly saw herself as a corpse and imagined herself laid out in a satin-lined coffin surrounded by flowers.

The dance floor was packed. Din red and blue spots lit the tables and bar, while the white bubble lights over the dance floor only added to the sepulchral atmosphere. Vida could feel that she needed to get the kinks out, needed to get herself moving before having to deal with Ramon Valdera. She had no trouble finding a partner.

Later in the evening, when the club was so full it was impossible to move through the crowd without attracting attention, she made her way to the rest room. Finding the metal box that held the main power switch, she wired it with a timer she had jury-rigged earlier that afternoon, and set it. Vida planned to plunge the club into darkness while, simultaneously, another gadget of her own manufacture set off a series of gunfire squibs beneath a table. Undoubtedly, Valdera's bodyguards would run over to investigate. At that moment she would be with the Cuban, ideally, in his arms. The gunshots would start a panic; customers would rush toward the door. The Cubans would be looking for a man with a gun and would pay no attention to her. By that time the Welrod would be back in her purse and she would simply walk out of the club and disappear.

There was just one problem: Ramon Valdera did not show up.

This Is Something New

THE NEXT MORNING GORO-
dish used the time afforded him by one of Alba's
flights of mysticism to take possession of the pagoda.
The place was silent, immaculate, a jewel box prepared to receive a gem of the Orient. It also smelled
of fresh paint, with a faint undertone of disinfectant.
Gorodish opened the windows. The sea air entered
and licked at the walls, ridding them forever of the
Swiss guru's odor of sanctity.

All in all, thought Gorodish, who was feeling
like the Dalai Lama, it wasn't a bad birthday present.

Seating himself in the center of the downstairs
room he listened to the ocean. Everything was perfect: he and Alba would each have an entire floor.
Yet, for some reason, Gorodish felt uneasy. Having
learned, from the Chinese philosophers, of the beauty
of nothingness he tried to figure the absolute minimum needed to furnish the house. Besides a piano,
that is. As far as sleeping arrangements went they
could choose anything they liked, from a hammock
to a water bed. Or, why not, a good old-fashioned
air mattress?

Gorodish decided to begin with the kitchen.

Going to a nearby telephone booth he quickly found out how one went about having the telephone, gas, electricity and water turned on. He also ordered a refrigerator-freezer with an automatic ice maker, and an energy-efficient, digitalized, computerized range. In white. After which he drove to a shopping mall and from among its hundred stores and boutiques bought a made-in-Italy metal table and garden chairs, white, red, yellow and blue plastic dishes, red-handled silverware, and enough pots and pans so that, if the urge took him, he might prepare a more elaborate meal than those they had been eating.

For lighting, he bought ten draftsman's lamps. He also purchased the longest white couch he had ever seen, a matte black Steinway and Sons grand piano, and a good television set. He did not buy a sound system. Perhaps it was Alba's influence but Gorodish suddenly wanted to limit the music in the house to what he, himself, could produce. To each his own asceticism.

What else did they need? Alba would no doubt have a few ideas of her own. He decided to leave her part of the house empty.

After trying a dozen beds Gorodish chose a Japanese-style beauty that, other than the perfection of its design, presented the advantage of fitting in with the generally Oriental theme of the pagoda. The bed consisted of a tatami platform, a *shikibhuton* and a *kakebhuton*, as well as a wheat-filled pillow. Buckwheat, according to the salesman. Gorodish was certain Alba would like it. Unless, of course, she decided to install a trapeze and inversion boots and sleep hanging upside down, like a bat.

Gorodish also bought a cordless telephone, a palm tree and a dish antenna that he intended to plant in the tiny backyard garden. The antenna could receive over one hundred television channels and he could think of no better way to subvert the Chinese.

The surprising thing was that by that evening everything was delivered and installed. Since the moving men could not get the Steinway up the narrow stairs Gorodish took the ground floor for himself. After plugging in the draftsman's lamps he moved the bed in front of the window so that it looked out over the ocean, then placed the enormous white couch in the center of the room where it immediately set up a vicious struggle with the black Steinway for control of the territory.

Exhausted, yet delighted with what he had accomplished, Gorodish sat down on the bench and, with a gesture of benediction, opened the piano. Not yet daring to touch it he stared at the black and white keys, then closed his eyes and waited for a work worthy of the instrument to emerge from his fingertips. When it came it turned out to be a piece by William Bird, its delicate structure slowly filling the room. Immobile at the piano, Gorodish felt the serenity and joy that only music, and Alba, could arouse in him.

To test the new cordless telephone, he punched in the number of the motel and the delightful voice of his hitchhiker on the road to enlightenment answered him.

"Have you reached an undifferentiated state?" he asked.

"I went for a swim."

"In the Tao?"

"The waves are very high. What did you do today?"

"I thought about you."

"Me, too, all day long. Will you be home soon?"

"Yes."

"Will you hold me in your arms?"

"Yes."

"Will you say sweet things?"

"Yes."

"I'll be waiting. Have you planned what we're going to do tomorrow?"

"I thought we might go to the movies."

"It's my birthday," Alba reminded him.

That's a Tango

DESPITE TRISTANA'S READ-ing, Vida returned to the Tropicana on Saturday and waited for a space to open up near the club before parking her Impala. Inside, the room was packed; it smelled of sweat and cheap perfume. Vida took a table near the door and ordered a glass of Wild Turkey. She was perspiring slightly, the palms of her hands moist. She did not yet know whether she would kill Ramon Valdera here: she would decide that when he showed up. While waiting, Vida danced a few tangos and kept a close watch on everything happening around her. None of Valdera's men had arrived.

She had decided that a timer was too undependable and had rigged the circuit breaker and gunshot squibs for remote control. She would be able to choose exactly the right moment to kill Valdera.

Vida chatted with several couples, maneuvering around them to place the explosive charges under the bar and near the table where Valdera usually sat. Later, after freshening her makeup, Vida wired the second remote-control device to the circuit breakers. The detonator was disguised as a button on her compact: all she would have to do is powder her nose.

At one in the morning the double doors swung open and two sides of beef entered. Thoroughly professional, they checked the room over, then stepped aside. Valdera came in, followed by a third bodyguard. Evidently his chauffeur had remained in the limousine parked out front.

Valdera was shown to his table. A bottle of champagne arrived there at the same time he did. Meanwhile the two sides of beef were examining every man in the room, their eyes as friendly as an oncologist tracking down a tumor. They glanced past Vida.

A few minutes later two girls in whose veins raced the combined fires of Africa and Jamaica showed up. After kissing Ramon, they sat down. He danced with one, then the other. Watching them, Vida saw that the girls would probably be wilder under satin sheets than they were here, performing the old-fashioned contortions to which Valdera was subjecting them. At their age they probably preferred getting it on to reggae. She felt somewhat reassured.

Pouting his displeasure, Valdera returned to his table and began force-feeding champagne to his female companions. All Vida had to do now was attract his attention.

Unscrupulously choosing the best dancer in the club, she pressed tightly against him and, finally, managed to inspire him with some of her own passion. Soon the other couples stopped dancing to watch. There came a moment when Vida could feel herself being dissected. She pretended not to notice, pushed her partner past the limits of his ability, then returned to her table.

First came the bottle of champagne, then came Valdera. Displaying all the arrogance and savoir faire that went with his position, he kissed her hand and asked permission to join her.

"You dance very well," he said. "It is a pleasure to watch you."

"Thank you," said Vida, gazing back at Valdera

with the exact same amount of arrogance, tinged with a hint of irony.

He could see she was testing him. Without a word he rose and held out his hand. Vida noticed the tattoo on the back of his knuckles, the identifying mark of a Cuban gang killer, one of the nastier Marielitos whom Castro had unloaded on the United States.

Valdera proved to be a better dancer than her other partners. After resisting slightly, just for the record, Vida let him lead. Proud of this first triumph, Valdera held her closely and tried to inject some warmth into his eyes, which were as sharp and cold as a big game hunter's arrows.

Valdera did not condescend to speak until after the seventh tango. "Are you a professional dancer?"

"No, but I love to dance."

"What else do you love?"

"Money, music, men."

"In that order?"

"It depends how I'm feeling at the time."

They sat down again. Vida was relieved: she had learned that Valdera had left his artillery in the cloakroom. His guardian angels, all three of whom were built like navy destroyers, never took their eyes from him.

Valdera called the waiter over and told him to remove the champagne flutes.

"It's estupid to drink champagne from little glasses. It's like a woman who wears a girdle."

The waiter placed oversized tulip-shaped wine-glasses on the table. "To let the champagne breathe," said Valdera, "to esmell the bouquet."

"That's why I prefer wine or bourbon," said Vida.

"What do you do?" Valdera demanded.

"I came here tonight because I don't feel like talking about myself," said Vida. "What do *you* do?"

"I'm in sugarcane."

"Are you from Argentina?" Vida asked naively.

"You got it right, baby. You know any other tango clubs in Los Angeles?"

"There used to be one downtown but it wasn't very good."

Opening her purse, Vida took out a small mirror and makeup kit. She brushed on some powder. Valdera turned away and she could sense his embarrassment. She patted at her makeup longer than necessary, wanting Valdera to become accustomed to the gesture.

"You one of those girls carries her whole wardrobe in her car?" he asked.

"No. But when I come to a neighborhood like this one I change into jeans, flats and a T-shirt before I go home." And a stun grenade, she thought, and a billy club.

"Esmart," said Valdera, smiling at her. It was probably the same exquisite smile he used when ordering that someone be chopped into tiny pieces.

They drank two more glasses of champagne. "You want to go to dinner?" Valdera's voice held implications for the rest of the evening.

"I'd like to dance a few more tangos, work up an appetite," said Vida.

The next time they sat down Valdera was out of breath. Pulling a handkerchief from the lapel pocket of his blue-striped gray silk suit, he elegantly mopped his forehead. On the far side of the dance floor his bodyguards appeared to have come to an understanding with the tropical chickies who had originally been with Valdera. The guards were looking less nervous now.

Vida and Ramon slopped down what was left of the champagne. She did a smoldering-passion number; Valdera strutted like a peacock waiting to shift into full display. Vida pulled out her makeup and checked her face again. Valdera's feathers drooped; prudishly, he turned his eyes away. She reached for the Welrod and pushed the remote-control button.

The room went black. All sound was drowned in the explosions coming from beneath the bar. Shouts. Screams. Vida threw herself into Valdera's arms for protection, pressed the Welrod against his heart, and pulled the trigger. At that moment she felt a knife penetrate her abdomen. She cried out. Valdera said nothing; he had already collapsed in her arms.

His fingers were still around the knife handle. Vida grasped his hand and, in one swift motion, pulled the blade free. She reloaded the Welrod then took the jeans from her handbag, rolled them around her fist and pressed them tightly against the wound in her belly.

The door was jammed with people trying to get out. Vida stood but the pain was so sharp her legs would not hold her. Dragging herself toward the doorway she suddenly found herself being carried along by the flood of customers pouring from the club. There was a man on the floor: it looked as if he had been trying to get into the nightclub, and there was an automatic in his hand. Probably the chauffeur. The crowd carried Vida toward him. She managed to raise the Welrod and, sliding it between two of the bodies pressing against her, fired. Ten feet away the chauffeur's head bounced backward, turned bloody and disappeared.

By propping herself against the parked cars Vida finally managed to reach the Impala. Opening the door, she sat down, refolded the bloodstained jeans and bound them to the wound with her belt. The pain was so intense now that even the light pressure of her foot on the accelerator was enough to make her cry out.

As she was driving away the first police cars arrived.

Tonight?

▲ GORODISH COULD FEEL PANIC gaining on him as he shopped for his nymph's birthday dinner. His legs felt weak so he bought lobsters, as if their exoskeletal firmness might rub off on him. Stopping at a liquor store he purchased champagne and a case of Wild Turkey: he would be needing it. On the way home he picked up a strawberry pie, asking the woman behind the counter to decorate it with fourteen birthday candles. As he watched her fold the pastry box Gorodish tried to imagine what his first night of love with Alba would be like. Luckily, the Cadillac was parked nearby. Gorodish tried to find courage in a quarter of a bottle of bourbon. The problem was that they'd put it off too long and he was now afraid that, when the moment came, he might find himself incapable.

The refrigerator was stocked with the sweet drinks his nymph liked best. When the third mayonnaise curdled, Gorodish decided to leave that part of the meal to Alba, set the table, swallowed a few tranquilizers, took a deep breath and, hand trembling, picked up the telephone.

"Hello, Alba. It's I."

"I know it's you: I recognized your voice. What're you doing?"

"I'm not too far away...."

"Come pick me up," she said. "Let's do something tonight. I don't want to have to wait until I'm menopausal to see a movie."

"No."

"What do you mean, no? Am I going to have to spend the night alone?"

"Leave the motel, turn right, and walk up the beach."

"How far? To San Francisco?"

"Until you feel like stopping."

"Sometimes you're not very romantic, you know?"

"Just do as I say."

Putting Chuang-tzu aside, Alba pulled a pair of jeans and a T-shirt over her swimsuit and left the motel. Following Gorodish's instructions, she walked north along the cement boardwalk that lay between the sand and the beach houses. There was no sign of Gorodish or the white Cadillac and she was beginning to wonder if he hadn't wanted her out of the motel room so that he might sneak in and prepare a surprise for her. After all, he wouldn't forget her birthday, would he?

Alba had been walking about ten minutes when she suddenly heard familiar music: some Bach thing or other. She kept on walking. It sounded like Gorodish playing, but since he had never recorded an album, it couldn't be. Alba turned her mind to Chuang-tzu again, then realized that the music box was actually an incredible Chinese pagoda. She began to wonder.

She walked up to the red lacquered door. It was open, so she entered and saw the space, the light, the bed, the white sofa, the table set for dinner, the black Steinway and, sitting at it, the craziest man she had ever met. Running over to Gorodish she climbed into his lap, placed her hands over his eyes and kissed him. Gorodish kept on playing, missing a few notes here and there, adding a few that didn't belong.

"Happy birthday," he said.

"You're my lemon sorbet, my California bitter orange, my African Eskimo Pie, my volcanic iceberg, my apple pan-Taody."

Cradling Alba in his arms, Gorodish rose from the piano.

"Show me the house," she ordered.

"You've already seen half of it," said Gorodish. "Now I'll show you the upstairs."

"I wonder what you've got up there."

"Close your eyes."

He deposited her in the middle of the upper room. Alba opened her eyes. "Fabulous," she said. "Better than anything I could ever imagine. How did you find it?"

"I was walking by, it was for sale, it was a steal."

"Simple."

"It's yours. You may do anything you want with it."

"We're going to live like postindustrial Taoist hermits."

They went back downstairs. "Could you make the mayonnaise?" asked Gorodish, somewhat embarrassed. "I've tried three times and it keeps separating."

"Are you nervous, my darling?"

"I don't know."

"Maybe you're having a 'midlife crisis,' as they say here."

"You think so?"

"It's possible."

"What is a 'midlife crisis'?"

"A sudden feeling of insecurity about one's masculinity, and an interest in young girls. I hope you're not going to cheat on me with someone younger than I am: that would be disgusting."

Gorodish smiled and opened a bottle of champagne. Alba whipped up a mayonnaise. "Should I add a touch of cayenne pepper?" she asked.

"Of course."

"It's so nice of you to have bought lobster."

"There's also a strawberry pie with birthday candles on it."

"Primo," said Alba losangelically. "Let's light them now so I can watch them burn. I don't want to be fourteen all at once: I want to make it last."

They sat down at the table and toasted each other, glasses clicking. During the meal they stood up several times to kiss: the table was too wide to reach across.

"You're looking pale, sweetheart," said Alba. "I think you've been working too hard. I can smell the fresh paint in here."

"I hired someone for that."

"Your hands are shaking."

"Jet lag. Change of altitude."

"I'm right: it's a midlife crisis."

"No, not at all."

"Oh, we're going to have fun here. Why aren't there any cassettes or records?"

"I've decided to make all my own music."

"I understand," said Alba. "The new piano is superb. Matte black *is* nicer, isn't it?"

As the white lobster meat disappeared Gorodish began acting strangely, going into the kitchen to bring back ice cubes, salt, anything else neither of them needed. Alba happily kept stuffing her face.

They opened the second bottle of champagne. Typhoon Alba blew out the candles. They sliced into the strawberry pie.

"Did you buy a Chinese bed?" she asked.

"Japanese," croaked Gorodish.

"That ought to be comfortable," said Alba. "Want to try it out?"

"Now?" he whispered

"Bring the bottle."

"Wouldn't you like to go out, take a ride in the Cadillac, visit a museum? There's an interesting exhibit of prehistoric weapons I thought you..."

"My dear Serge, museums are closed at night and

you know I don't give a damn about prehistoric weapons."

"True. Why don't you go to bed and I'll play something for you?"

"I'd like that."

Alba stood and let her clothes slip to the floor. Gorodish stared at her, then turned and stalked toward the piano. He began with *The Well-Tempered Clavier*, a long piece, something that would buy him some time. He even invented variations of his own. (Once, in a translation, he had seen the title rendered as "The Clavichord with the Right Temperature.")

Sliding into the futon, Alba uttered ecstatic little moans. It sounded to her as if Gorodish was playing at a rather more languid tempo than usual. Probably the effect of all the alcohol he had drunk. Alba conscientiously emptied the champagne bottle and let the music take her.

Inspired, Gorodish next played *The Goldberg Variations*, another long work with much room for improvisation. Alba accompanied him, humming her own version of the version by Glenn Gould, one of Gorodish's heroes.

It was almost three in the morning when Gorodish finally walked across the room and approached the sacrificial altar. But first there was one last delay for a side trip to the refrigerator where he popped open the last bottle of champagne and thought of all the Japanese who, at one time or another, had deliberately stepped onto a tatami mat in preparation for committing *suppuku*.

He had expected Alba to be asleep but she was waiting for him, eyes wide open.

"You play so beautifully. I adore the piano."

"Do you want to hear something else?" he offered. "*The Diabelli Variations? Das Hammerklavier?*"

"No. Come here."

Gorodish undressed and got into bed. Alba put her arms around him. "Do you want me to take charge?" she asked.

"That's about all I can do at this point," Gorodish said, his voice trembling.

"You're scared to death," said Alba. "Don't try to hide it."

"Yes."

"Me, too." She caressed Gorodish's hair, his forehead. "I've asked myself so many questions and I'm not sure I have the answers. Could you help me?" she said sweetly.

"Maybe."

"If we start making love, will we be able to stop?"

"Probably not."

"That's what I thought. We'd probably spend twenty hours a day in the sack trying everything, like two crazy people."

"No doubt."

"We wouldn't have time for anything else."

"No. At least, not for a while."

"Six months."

"Yes."

"It would screw up my search for spiritual enlightenment."

"It might."

"I think it would. You know, all the books I've read say that converting sexual energy into spiritual energy is the best way to make progress. . . ."

"The Chinese are usually right. They've been trying things for thousands of years."

"Even if it isn't true, maybe we could . . ."

"Yes, my darling, whatever you want."

"But we've both been waiting for this for so long."

"Yes."

"Maybe we could wait a little while longer? We could think of this as a moment of *in-action*. I mean, we'll do it, eventually, but then it will be action and won't have to carry the added burden of so much spirituality. . . ."

"That's a wonderful idea."

"You're not disappointed?"

"No. You?"

"I don't think so. Anyway, if we ever really want to do it we can always change our minds."

They kissed until sun filled the pagoda. "That was the most wonderful night we've ever had," Alba whispered ecstatically.

"Yes, my darling. You're so sweet."

"I feel as if I've merged with the Tao."

"Do you?"

"Yes. I can't feel a thing. I'm floating, soaring. It's magic."

They slept for seventeen hours with Alba's body

draped across Gorodish, he holding her in his arms.
When they awoke she straddled him and said,
"When someone merges with the Tao he can do
anything he wants, right? Every action is perfect,
right?"

"I think so," said Gorodish, wondering at the
frown on his nymph's face.

"Good. You know all the reading I've been doing?
I counted them: fifty-eight books. Now I think it's
time for some action."

"You mean . . ." said Gorodish as tentatively as
an astronaut taking his first step on Nymphela.

"No," laughed Alba. "I woke up ten minutes ago
filled with the sudden desire to be a private detective. Now, if Los Angeles isn't the place for it, I
don't know where is. One ought to follow one's
impulses, don't you agree?"

"A private detective?"

"Like Marlowe."

"It's a lousy job," said Gorodish. "And it doesn't
pay very well."

"It does if you're a genius at it."

"Where will you find clients?"

"I found you, didn't I?"

"Yes, but business is different."

"You have no faith in me."

"As a seductress, yes; as a private detective, I'm
not so sure. It's dangerous. And you'd need an office,
a license . . ."

"I know," said Alba, "and a gat, luck, clients,
venetian blinds, a bottle of bourbon, a snap-brim

hat, a raincoat and a roadster. Listen, times have changed: I want to do this in a more contemporary style."

"All right," said Gorodish, "I'll try to set it up for you."

"I'm going to call my detective agency Pink and Pink."

"Bizarre."

"You like Erton and Erton better?"

"No."

"Let's go buy some croissants, pick up our things from the motel and plan our future."

Body and Soul

FOR THE LAST TEN MINUTES Vida had been floating down the freeway, the car wandering like a motorboat that had loosed its moorings. The Shrine Auditorium drifted into view, the Wagnerian grandiosity of its white domes evoking visions of a paradise in which Dillinger waited to welcome her with open arms. Vida swam off the freeway, took Hoover Avenue, turned left and brought the car to a stop in the middle of a lawn.

In better days the wood-frame house had been white, its spindle columns an exquisite example of the neo-Bavarian style as seen through the eyes of an Arcologist. Lianas gripped the house tightly, as if to keep it from falling, and termites could be heard jawing from thirty feet away, no doubt discussing the collapse of Western civilization.

Vida did not even have the strength to turn off the motor or lift her foot from the accelerator. The Impala's headlights pierced through the front porch latticework and shone on Sean, who was drinking a Budweiser and watching the Playboy channel.

Sean came out on the porch. Vida was sitting with her forehead pressed against the steering wheel. He recognized her profile through the side window, then saw the blood. His legs turned to Dacron. Livid, he touched her hair, saying, "Vida, what happened? We have to get you to a hospital."

"No, please, we've got to keep this a secret. You take care of me."

"I don't have any supplies here."

"What about at school?"

Sean was pale. "You've lost a lot of blood," he said hesitantly. "I'd have to get a pass from a friend of mine, and I don't have the keys. . . ."

Vida gathered what remained of her strength and shouted, "Just do it!" Then she fainted.

I Don't Have a License

HOPING TO FIND SOMEONE willing to take a neophyte Marlowe under his wing Gorodish and Alba visited every detective agency listed in the Yellow Pages. They were greeted with laughter or demands for extortionate amounts of money.

Toward the end of their search they came across an old-timer named Max Van Ness. Gorodish telephoned before they drove over. A tired voice said, "Van Ness Private Investigations. What can I do for you?"

"I want to see you."

"Nothing easier: I'm not the president. Office hours are from nine to five."

Ten minutes later they walked into a tiny wood bungalow that, in earlier days, had been a hamburger stand. The old sign, its letters bleached by the sun, was still visible on one wall.

A small, yellowed square of peeling plastic bore the name VAN NESS. Night-blooming jasmine swarmed over a roofed patio where Max Van Ness reclined on a chaise longue. He must have been seventy, his face something out of Dante's *Inferno*, his eyes those of a sociopathic bloodhound. Built like a second-rate Robert Mitchum, his thick lips were curled around a Mexican cigar.

Van Ness rose and kicked the door shut. "Come in," he said amiably.

Inside the one-room cottage were three easy chairs which had probably been new at about the time of the Bear Flag Republic, a pot from which came the tantalizing aroma of Kilimanjaro-grown coffee beans, a small steel desk covered with papers and a baseball bat. This last seemed to fascinate Gorodish.

"Just in case someone breaks in," said Van Ness who, when seated at his desk, could reach everything in the room.

"I have a business deal for you," said Gorodish.

"I only kill in self-defense."

"You misunderstand."

"No, I don't . . . believe me, this job doesn't pay very well. You earn just enough to get by, sometimes."

"I'd like to buy half your company," said Gorodish. Pointing at Alba he added, "You need a partner."

"My company? Who do you think you're talking to: American Express?"

"You wouldn't want to discourage young talent, would you?"

Van Ness smiled tenderly at Alba. "Girlie," he said, "you may think there's a gold mine in this business but you could wind up with lead in your pretty little butt."

Taking a glass jar from a drawer, he handed it to Alba. The jar held thirty bullets, some flattened, others intact.

"Your vitamins?" asked Alba.

"That's what they've dug out of me in my forty-eight years in this business. And I won't bore you by mentioning the dents in my skull, the stuff I've had to swallow, the three cars that exploded, two of them with my partners inside, the other with my wife. I've been thrown into lake and ocean, tossed from a plane in flight and now, at my age, when I should be taking it easy, maybe fishing for marlin in Mexico, I'm still out there following some bimbo jogging with her boyfriend, or doing all the work and letting the cops take the credit. And the bastards won't even cover me when I get into trouble."

"Fishing season opens tomorrow," said Gorodish, pulling a sheaf of thousand-dollar bills from his pocket.

Van Ness lifted the money to a nose with nostrils so cavernous they looked as if he spent his spare time picking them with cigars.

"Smells good, even if it *is* only paper."

"A small down payment," said Gorodish. "You cover the kid with your license; officially, we say she's your operative. All I want is a phone number where she can reach you if she needs advice."

"The offer's so good I won't even bother counting the money. This isn't some stupid TV show like *Candid Camera*, is it? I've got a heart condition."

"Come have dinner at our pagoda," said Alba.

"Closing time," Van Ness announced jovially. "Baja's only a day's drive away. I'll send you snapshots of everything I catch."

"What would you like for dinner?" Alba asked.

"How about some tuna, just to get things rolling."

"Let's go shopping," said Gorodish. "Do you think you can teach a highly motivated student the basics of your profession in one evening?"

"It's very simple," said Van Ness. "The main thing is to avoid getting killed. Everything else follows."

Taking a key ring from his pocket he unhooked the key to the bungalow. "Here, Miss Detective, it's all yours." He tossed the key to Alba, who caught it in midair.

"How do you use that?" Alba asked, pointing at the baseball bat.

Van Ness's hand whipped out and seized the bat. Using Gorodish as a visual aid he pointed to the vulnerable areas of the human body. "Shins, knees, balls, shoulders and head. One whack ought to do it, if you hit hard enough."

"I think I'll take up the martial arts."

"The only problem with that is your average bullet travels nine hundred feet per second. This time tomorrow I'll be in Tijuana and the day after, I'll be fishing! But I promise to lease a boat with a ship-to-shore telephone."

Doc. Thanks
for the Time.

SEAN PARKED BEHIND THE Hoffman Research Center building at the USC School of Medicine. Vida was still unconscious. He carried her into the Animal Tower and took the elevator to the subterranean operating rooms.

Closing the blinds he turned on the lights over the table. Sean began by injecting Vida with dextromoramide tartrate, following that with a shot of succinylcholine so that her intestines wouldn't hit the ceiling when he opened her. The main risk now was peritonitis: he would have to examine her closely and pray that the knife had not touched her intestines.

If another doctor or one of the security guards caught him it would be the end of his medical career. Sean cut Vida open with a single sweep of the scalpel: a real pro.

Miraculously, Valdera's blade had slipped between the convolutions of Vida's intestines without touching them. Sean wiped away the perspiration beading his forehead, then put everything back neatly before carefully sewing her up again.

It Would Have Cost a Hundred Bucks to Wash the Windows

PHARAOH TREATED HIMSELF TO lunch at the Bellevue, which had been Thomas Mann's favorite restaurant. Then he had a taxi drive him around Encino while he thought back to the time, eighteen years earlier, when he had prowled Los Angeles armed with a Rolleiflex. Finding the mansion had been a shock: pseudo-English, Chandler had called it. The house had had everything: landscaped grounds and gardens, conical roofs, even a caretaker's cottage, a smaller version of the main house.

Pharaoh could not recall exactly where the house was. The taxi drove around for a good hour before the peaked roofs appeared from behind a stand of trees.

He paid the driver, pushed open the gate and walked up the driveway. The house looked empty. The lawn had not been mowed in a long while and the garden was overgrown. The property was both hideous and marvelous at the same time, its architectural style nothing more than an accumulation of the expensive materials that had gone into the building of it. The place was perfect for an actor gone senile, yet Pharaoh could feel his adolescent enthusiasm for it coming alive. Just as he had decided the house was uninhabited, a fat man came out onto the front porch.

"You looking for something?" The tone was not friendly.

"I'm sorry, I thought the house was empty. This place brings back old memories."

"Did the agency send you?"

"Why? Is the house for sale?"

"For rent, under certain conditions."

"I'm interested."

"Come in." After examining him closely the man said, "There's no real-estate agency fee, and no lease. You can pay me in cash, five thousand dollars for one month."

"I'll take it."

"Everything works. The rent includes gas, electricity and the telephone charges up to two hundred dollars. There's a gate in the back fence that leads to a shopping center. You won't even have to drive."

"It's exactly what I've been looking for," said Pharaoh staring at a heavy metal door. "What's in there?"

"The security system. There's three separate systems for the house, and a magnetic field surrounding the garden. You don't have to use it if you don't want to."

"Oh, I rather like playing around with buttons and switches."

"An Italian decorator did the house. You don't often find a place . . ."

"I recognize the style," Pharaoh said dryly. Most of the furniture and objets d'art were fakes, executed with the consummate artistry found only among Neapolitan counterfeiters.

The owner left. Pharaoh began laughing hysterically: he had never dreamed that one day he would find himself surrounded by so much bad taste. He tried to add up how much the owner had paid. Whoever the decorator had been, he seemed to have furnished everything, including the doorknobs. Pharaoh's natural instincts would normally have led him to a cheap motel in Hollywood, or to a small cottage at the beach. There he might have spent his time developing new theories of architecture; instead he found himself isolated from the world and living in a sort of fortress that fairly reeked of new money with nothing in it to hold his interest except, perhaps, a few dust puffs.

Pharaoh examined the house thoroughly, each room arousing in him the exact same amount of anxiety. The bathroom faucets were gold-plated; even the beds had been made. Towels, bath salts and cologne had been provided. A volume on fifteenth-century Catholicism lay open on the desk in the library; obviously it, too, came with the house, as did a collection of Italian literary classics in gold-stamped leather bindings. Pharaoh searched for a book by his favorite author. In vain.

As a gesture of rebellion against his surroundings

Pharaoh decided that he would eat very simply. Crossing the garden he found the small door in the fence and, beyond it, the shopping center. A health food store faced the parking lot. Pharaoh went in and bought ten pounds of brown rice, soybean sprouts, carrot and boysenberry juice, seven-grain bread and honey. The one thing he could not deprive himself of, however, was coffee.

A pale, diffident little man waited on him, bowing respectfully each time he placed an item on the counter. Despite his fame Pharaoh had never become accustomed to such deference.

"It's nice that another celebrity's going to be living in that house," said the little gray man, taking a puff on his huge cigar. "May I recommend a rare tea we import directly from Hong Kong?"

"Ginseng?"

"Yes, mixed with several herbs reputed to renew one's energy. Yet it may be drunk at night and will cause no problems for one's sleep."

"I'll take some," said Pharaoh.

"Did you want this delivered?"

"Don't bother."

The little gray man handed Pharaoh a business card. "If you need anything please don't hesitate to call. It's been a pleasure serving you."

Half an hour later Pharaoh was seated in an armchair, reading a paperback edition of the complete works of Raymond Chandler. The television was on. From time to time he looked up to catch a glimpse of some unpretentiously rotten set design.

The evening news came on. Pharaoh watched it distractedly for a while, then turned up the sound to hear a report of the day's crimes and court trials. He had always had a fondness for the caricatures of alleged perpetrators, the pathetic sketches of the accused that were shown in place of videotapes or photographs. An anchorwoman described the opening day of the trial of a man who claimed to have killed more than three hundred people. After which, rearranging her face into a more serious expression, she described a police artist's sketch as it was flashed on the screen.

"After an eight-year investigation, the FBI now believes this to be the Welrod Killer. According to FBI spokesperson, this woman has allegedly murdered twenty-seven people, including Ramon Valdera, reputed head of a Cuban drug ring, who was found dead in a Watts nightclub last Saturday morning. A description of the killer has been furnished to the police by Valdera's bodyguards. The Cuban mobster's body was found with a bloodstained knife in its hand, leading the FBI to believe that the woman, with whom Valdera had been dancing, is seriously wounded.

"FBI sources admit that they would not have been able to link Valdera's death to the earlier twenty-six murders if the killer had not used a Welrod, a gun originally developed in Britain during World War Two. The use of such an exotic and easily identified weapon is rare among professional killers, and is considered by police to be a major clue in the case. The Los Angeles Police Department states that it hopes to identify the Welrod Killer within the next few days.

"With the police, FBI, and the Cuban drug syndicate on the lookout for her, and considering the seriousness of her wounds, there is little chance the killer will strike again in the Los Angeles area."

The anchorwoman gazed into the camera lens with a fatalistic smile.

What a fascinating person, thought Pharaoh as, alone in the solitude of his golden prison, he stirred a pot of brown rice. Later he ate the rice slowly and waited for the six o'clock news. Pharaoh wanted to know more about the mysterious killer.

Pink & Pink

THE NEXT TIME GORODISH SAW the bungalow it was pink and Alba was lolling on the chaise longue, a neon sign above her head adding a touch of raspberry syrup to the confection.

"Well, Miss Detective, how's business?"

"I think Max got the better part of the deal."

"You have to go out and drum up business. Solve one or two cases and word of mouth will do the rest. May I look inside?"

"Nothing's been changed. I thought it would look more authentic as it was."

Gorodish poured himself a cup of coffee, then sat down beside his nymph.

"You're looking a little depressed, honeybunch," said Alba. "Are you taking Valium again?"

"Only four a day. I've been a little nervous lately."

"How would you like to help me?"

"No. I'm practicing my piano. Help you do what?"

"I don't know, but something will turn up."

"You ought to advertise."

"I've already bought ten thousand dollars worth of ad space. I know it's not very much but I want to feel my way into the business."

"How does your ad read?"

"Help Fade Crime With Pink and Pink."

"Not bad."

"You'll see. I'll have wall-to-wall clients in no time."

"You ought to watch television and read the newspapers," Gorodish suggested. "You can never tell, something might catch your eye."

"This is the age of the computer, old friend," said Alba, planting a perfumed kiss on his mouth. "Why don't you go back to your Godowsky études."

The Cadillac headed back toward the ocean. Alba sipped a strawberry shake and thought of the old Chinese Sages. A white limousine drew up in front of her pastry. A chauffeur opened the rear door and something resembling bananas and cream got out.

"Horace Perceval Third, president of Biz and Biz."

"Alba, president of Pink and Pink."

"I knew it the moment I saw you. Do you mind if we talk in my car? I'm expecting an important phone call."

The chauffeur closed the door. Inside was a snug, silent world containing a television set, a computer terminal, two telephones, a bar with spigots for coffee and Coca-Cola, and air conditioning turned up so high that Alba felt as if she were sitting in vanilla ice cream.

"How did you know I was the owner of Pink and Pink?"

"Something about your ad felt familiar. Genius tends to disappear with the onset of adolescence; I plan to retire on my fifteenth birthday. How much do you charge?"

"Three hundred a day, plus expenses."

"All right. If you solve the case I'll give you one hundred thousand as a bonus."

"I get a week's fee in advance."

"You're to drop everything else you're working on," said Horace Perceval III.

"Why don't you just tell me your problem?"

"A genius has disappeared. He happens to be my father. You're the only one I've told. Of course I don't want the police involved: they're so heavy-handed. I expect you to be fast, subtle and discreet. Here's your week in advance." Horace Perceval handed Alba several thousand-dollar bills. "Do you have a computer?"

"No."

"I'll have one installed for you with a modem to link you to my data bank. I'll also provide you with a complete file on my father. I'll want detailed reports as your investigation proceeds. I'm available twenty-four hours a day. My people will be here in an hour and . . ."

The telephone rang. Horace Perceval III picked up the receiver. His hand was trembling.

"We've bought it," said the voice on the phone.

"Congratulations."

"Shall we put it back on the market?"

"No. It's for my personal collection." Horace Perceval III was jubilant. "I've just purchased the original Rosebud at the Sotheby auction."

"Congratulations," said Alba with her most delicious smile.

"If my father takes a liking to you I'm sure he'll design something outrageous for you. If you find him I may even pay to build it. *Mi piramide es su piramide,*" said Horace Perceval III, handing her his card.

They shook hands vigorously. Alba went back to her chaise longue and began counting dollars.

Technicians came, installed a computer terminal and showed her how to use it. A half hour later Alba watched as the file on Pharaoh scrolled up the display screen. A printer clattered as it produced hard copy of those items she thought important.

At one in the morning a dumbfounded Gorodish

entered the bungalow. "I see you're starting out big," he said.

"My first client," said Alba. "It's an important account."

The printer was delivering a computerized portrait of a man. Gorodish looked at it and murmured, "I'll say it's an important account: Marlowe Wrightson, the Pharaoh himself."

"My client's name is Horace Perceval III. Not a bad kid: ten years old, a millionaire, president of a company called Biz and Biz. He's just bought the *Citizen Kane* sled. I think we're going to get along very nicely. Here's his first payment." Alba flashed a green fan of money.

"And the computer?"

"He had it put in so we can exchange information more quickly."

"You *have* made a good start," said Gorodish, washing down his fifth Valium of the day with a cup of Kilimanjaro coffee.

"Why would someone like Pharaoh disappear? Do you think he's been kidnapped?"

Gorodish did not answer. The night was warm and fragrant but he was already immersed in the file on Pharaoh.

Nice and Quiet
Here

WHEN NOT READING, PHA-
raoh wandered through the house and grounds. The
Welrod Killer was constantly on his mind. While
eating his brown rice he scanned the papers for news,
imagining her on the move from one hideout to
another as she fled both Cuban killers and the police.
Nothing was known of her private life or, perhaps,
the press was not telling all it knew. Pharaoh wondered if her body had not already been dumped
where it would not be found for months.

At night he played with the security system until
it became obvious that even a stray cat wandering
across the grounds was enough to set it off. He
could feel himself slipping into a nervous breakdown. In his dreams he grew ill at the very sight
of a straight line and, waking in a sweat, left the
house and roamed the city only to find himself
forced to face its abominable buildings, all straight
lines and right angles. He began to perceive rectilinearity as vile and sensed that never again would
his hand respond as it had. It came to him that the
straight line was an insult to Nature, a sort of per-
version of the human spirit, and he began to feel a

growing disgust for that corruption in his earlier works.

After a while Pharaoh began to dream of buildings made exclusively of curves. As he meditated on the engineering problems one might encounter in the construction of such buildings, elegant solutions began to occur to him. Going to a shopping center he bought a large sketchpad and pencils. As he began drawing curves he was almost overcome by the thought of all those other, loathsome architects, and of a city overrun by their rectilinear monstrosities.

That night he learned more about his new idol. An FBI snitch had noticed the amazing resemblance between the police artist's sketch and a local nightclub owner. Twelve minutes later the FBI's computer file on Vida was on the local news, and she was famous. Her name screamed from headlines. Bit by bit, the most intimate details of her life were made public. Jazz musicians appeared on TV, weeping as they described her generosity and her contributions to the development and preservation of the art of jazz, the only indigenous American art form, and a dying one, it was pointed out.

Reporters were on the scent. Photographs of the club, and of the modest apartment above it, appeared everywhere. Complete details of the preceding twenty-seven murders were reported, repeated, rehashed. Experts explained the history and proper use of the Welrod. Childhood snapshots of Vida were dug up from somewhere. Radio stations began playing the Charlie Parker cut on which her mother's wonderful, hoarse voice could be heard.

Under the overall title "Lady Sings the Death Blues," the *Los Angeles Times* published a series of articles covering Vida's life story; the series was syndicated.

By now the public was openly sympathetic to a killer whose victims had all been gangsters or corrupt politicians. In the black community prayers for Vida's safe escape were offered in neighborhood churches. A well-known New York writer announced he was writing a docunovel about the woman he called "one of the great heroines of contemporary American history."

Magazine articles revealed that several jazz festivals had received supposedly anonymous donations, nightclub owners had been saved from bankruptcy by last-minute cash miracles, and jazz albums had been financed by the woman jazz musicians and fans alike were now calling "Big Mama." Penniless young musicians reported that they had been given better instruments on which to practice, or money for tuition, while their wives had received help with household expenses. The FBI admitted that the financing behind a well-known detox center had been traced to the mysterious Vida.

A major Hollywood film company signed thirty writers to collaborate on a screenplay recounting the fabulous life and times of Vida. Politicians began offering their opinions on the matter.

Schoolchildren paraded through Watts carrying

signs reading KEEP YOUR ASS DOWN, VIDA. For several days there was no gang violence.

Songwriters wrote ballads and pop singers miaowed them, while the Los Angeles police nervously fingered their sidearms. In West Hollywood the men kept on dancing. Determined that the institution not die each night, the great jazz musicians gathered at Ornithology to jam.

A Tree Moving Gently Against a Hazed Blue Sky

DAYS LATER VIDA OPENED her eyes and saw a tree moving gently against a hazed blue sky. There was an IV bottle, a bandage around her abdomen and pain when she moved her legs. She recognized Sean's house and felt safe for a moment. Then she realized she was alone.

On a table next to the bed was a penciled note:

Vida,
   Don't worry. Your wound is healing. There's no internal damage. Don't be afraid. I know what you did, there was a police sketch of you on TV. You're safe here. If you want to, you can leave in a few days.

                                        Love,
                                        Sean

Vida tried to stay calm. If Sean had wanted to turn her in to the police she would not have awakened here, in his house. Raising up on one elbow she peeked outside. Her car was not there. She hoped Sean had hidden it in the garage. It was good to be back, even though Los Angeles was probably a beehive of activity, humming with cops and Cubans, with Vida the queen.

Hot Stuff

PHARAOH ADDED A FEW mushrooms to his brown rice, then sat down in front of the television set to eat. Like thousands of other viewers he feared that an FBI agent, or a cop, might soon proudly announce Vida's arrest or, given her reputation, her death. No doubt credit for her capture would be shared equally between the Cubans and the LAPD. But the evening's news was reassuring: the Vida phenomenon was still growing even though the heroine herself could not be found.

The telephone rang. Pharaoh hesitated, then answered.

"Can I come over now?" a young man's voice asked.

"Of course," Pharaoh heard himself say.

"In half an hour?"

"Fine."

While waiting for his mysterious visitor Pharaoh drank a large glass of carrot juice. He could feel the torpor into which he had been sinking beginning to dissipate. A car drew up outside and Pharaoh stepped out onto the porch to greet his guest.

"Please come in."

The man's name was Enrico Tor. Opening the trunk of his Buick Regal, he lifted out something that looked like a painting wrapped in canvas, and carried it into the house. Leading the way into the living room, Pharaoh opened the fake-Renaissance bar, saying, "Would you care for a drink?"

"Scotch, please."

"May I see the painting?"

"It's worth a bundle, but it's hot. I need to leave it here until things cool down."

"We haven't met before, have we?"

"No, but the guy who lived here before you was real cooperative. He was, uh, on vacation, too."

Pharaoh went into the kitchen for ice while Tor unwrapped the canvas. It was a magnificent Malevich.

Visibly intimidated by his treasure Tor said, "You like it?"

"Oh, I don't know that much about painting. . . ."

"Can you keep it for me until I make a deal on it?"

"Take down the nymphs and put this one up,"

said Pharaoh. "It's more . . . modern. When do you think you'll be back?"

"In a month, maybe. I'm from Las Vegas. The cops were getting too close so nobody from the family would help me."

"I understand."

Twenty-four Hours a Day Somebody Is Running

IT WAS HOT, THE AIR HEAVY; Vida walked, one hand poised to grab the gun in her cotton tote bag. She was confident, as she usually was when in danger, knowing that sooner or later something would turn up.

She walked three blocks, up side streets lined with dilapidated houses, heading for the Santa Monica Freeway.

Outside a weatherbeaten wood-frame house a young black man was polishing an almost new Japanese motorcycle. Through an open door Vida could see a television set and a sagging couch.

The young man was whistling "Naima," by John Coltrane. She walked over and sat down on the porch steps.

"Evening," she said.

"Evenin," the young man smiled.

"I heard you whistling 'Naima.' That's one of my favorites."

"You like jazz?"

"Yes."

For the first time the young man looked directly at her. His heart began to pound like a 750-cc engine.

"You're Vida . . . I saw you on . . ."

"Yes."

"They say they're gettin close to findin you. They say it's a matter of hours."

"It's always just a matter of hours."

"You goin to kill me?"

Vida smiled, moved over to him and affectionately ran her fingers through his long, tightly curled hair. "I don't do that unless I'm paid."

"Everybody at school's talkin about you, about how you done a whole lot for jazz."

"What are you studying to be?"

"Movie editor."

"That's good."

"This is like a mirage or somethin; for a minute I thought I been smokin too much grass. Can I touch you?"

"Of course."

"You hurt bad?"

"I'm all right now."

"Folks're worried about you."

"I've heard."

"You need somethin? You want to stay awhile?"

"I don't want to put anyone in danger, but I'll

need your bike for a while, and a helmet, if you have one."

"I got a brand-new one; you can have it."

"You'll get it back."

"Really?"

"Believe it."

"Okay, if you say so. You want my leathers, too? Nobody's goin to be recognizin you if you wearin my leathers."

"I'll call you, tell you where you can pick up your bike."

"I just filled the tank."

"What's your name?"

"Jay."

"Thanks, Jay."

The living room was filled with books on film. Jay brought out his leather jeans and jacket, and his new helmet. Vida pulled them on over the jeans and T-shirt she had borrowed from Sean.

"What's goin to happen to your club?"

"The police'll probably close it."

"There's been sessions there every night, for free. Too bad you can't hear them. Folks say it's hot, everybody been showin up to play. I'm goin there tomorrow night."

"Ask for Doug," said Vida, "a friend of mine who's there every night. Tell him I'm okay and ask him to get some money together. I don't have a cent on me."

"I don't have much but I could maybe let you have fifty."

"Okay. If anything happens to your bike Doug'll see you get reimbursed."

Vida kissed Jay on the cheek, pulled on the helmet and climbed onto the motorcycle.

"I'll call you in about an hour," she said, then disappeared into the night.

Two Leeches in a White Cadillac

AFTER MANY HOURS OF staring at the computer terminal screen Alba's eyes had become so tired that she had even caught a glimpse of the Immortals dancing against the darkening sky. Now she sat, one hand on Gorodish's thigh, her feet propped up against the *grande crème's* dashboard. The Cadillac glided smoothly along the Santa Monica Freeway, wind caressing her face, long, serpentine curves soothing not only Ms. Pink but the depressed elephant beside her.

"I need a change, something new," said Alba.

"Do you want to go back to the pagoda?"

"Why don't we take a drive?"

"Up Pacific Coast Highway, to Santa Barbara?"

Beyond Malibu, where sumptuous shanties seemed to be sliding into the ocean, stars appeared. The road ran parallel to the beach, rising steadily then falling until it was level with the sand.

"We could drive north all the way to the Inuit," said Alba.

"I think the road's blocked below Big Sur."

"Maybe that's where the Pharaoh's hiding. Or maybe he's been kidnapped."

"Nobody kidnaps a genius."

"Stop here. I want to listen to the ocean."

Gorodish eased back on the accelerator and the Cadillac came to rest at the side of the road, like a huge albino shark stranded on the sand. Sitting at either end of the wide front seat they could feel the fins trembling in the night.

A single headlight jerked them from their reverie. The young motorcycle cop walked over to the car. "You can't park here."

"I'm having a religious experience," said Alba with all the charm she could muster.

"Why don't you folks go to a motel?"

"We're leaving," Gorodish said politely.

It took them a good ten minutes to recapture the precop mood.

"I don't see why Horace Perceval Third's so worried about his father," said Gorodish. "Pharaoh's probably gone off somewhere to search for a hidden treasure chamber."

"You think he's in Egypt?"

"His own brain's all the Egypt that man needs.

His sort doesn't even need a plane in order to fly."

"Maybe he's in a motel room somewhere, shooting up," suggested Alba. "In his own way, Pharaoh's something of a Taoist."

"I thought the Immortals needed no drug but the Tao."

"Not true," said Alba. "They liked to get drunk, too. They lived in hermitages set on riverbanks or near lakes, enchanted settings in which they wrote poems and discussed Indifferentiation."

"I'm starting to like your Taoists," said Gorodish, "but what I'm really interested in now is this Vida business."

"There's no accounting for taste," said Alba. "Even if the Cubans or cops haven't found her yet, I don't think she'd be out here, thumbing a ride up Pacific Coast Highway."

At dawn, tired but happy, Gorodish and Alba returned to the pagoda and broke their fast in the kitchen.

"You know," said Alba, "I don't have a bed of my own."

"Do you want me to buy you one?"

"I'm afraid to leave you on your own for even a minute," she said. "I'm afraid you're going to do a Hugo Wolff on me: I don't want you to go gaga."

Holding Gorodish in her arms, she caressed his face until his breathing was deep and regular. Then Alba slipped from the futon and jogged all the way back to Pink & Pink. She was about to open the door when a truck passed by; there was just time enough for her to read the blue letters on a white background:

CHANDLER BAKERY

Taking it as a sign from the Immortals, Alba starting combing through the Master's work in hopes of spotting the outline of a pyramid, the shadow of a pharaoh, hidden somewhere between two metaphors. After rereading the dossier one last time she came to the conclusion that it was time to prove herself worthy of Marlowe so she ordered the computer to print out all the data it had on Chandler.

After three hours of intense concentration she sat down at the computer again and typed the following message:

"HP3:

Did Pharaoh leave pyramid empty-handed? Where is *The Long Goodbye*? If missing pls send printout all houses photographed/mentioned in thesis."

Do You Love Me Very Much?

BILL HATED AIR CONDITION-
ing. Preferring the street smells, he spent his nights
in a wicker armchair just inside the main gate of
the studio where he worked as a watchman. A former bass player, Bill resembled a bronze sculpture,
one now conscientiously chewing on a ketcup-
drenched hamburger whose cucumber and tomato
slices had a tendency to escape from the bun. Grip-
ping the dripping burger in one large hand he con-
templatively sucked on a straw jammed into a giant
paper goblet filled with shaved ice and Coca-Cola.
Finished eating, Bill wiped his right hand on his
dirty trousers, stretched, lit a cigarette and glanced
down in disgust at the small, scratchy radio sitting
on the ground next to the empty soft-drink con-
tainer. Like ninety percent of the city's black pop-
ulation Bill was worried that Vida might fall into
one of the many traps the police had set for her.
He was a regular at Ornithology, spending his free
nights there listening to the sounds and sipping
bourbon.

A motorcycle pulled up beside him. Vida raised
the helmet visor. Bill was not surprised: having

converted to Islam almost twenty years earlier, he knew that the Prophet took a personal interest in important matters.

"I was hoping I'd find you," said Vida.

He led her into the deserted studio. "I'm like a ol alley cat," said Bill, "always out there on the street."

"I need a place to sleep."

"There's a mattress in the storeroom; sometimes the guys'll catch a nod."

"Dial this phone number, would you? The boy's name is Jay. He'll come pick up his motorcycle. Here are the keys."

"I'm glad you came to me. I been prayin for you."

"Thanks, Bill. Is anybody coming in tomorrow morning?"

"Just a little ol rock group, got no licks; gonna put them in Studio Five. Don't you worry. I'll take care of you."

"Wake me in forty-eight hours. You have a car?"

"Just the same ol pile of junk."

Do You Know How They Shoot Tigers?

EACH TIME HE WALKED PAST the Malevich it shook him to the depths of his being, shook him so badly that he began to question his sudden distaste for rectilinearity.

Pharaoh studied his new sketches. The old Russian master's straight lines had begun chipping away at his new passion for curves. The painting was becoming an obsession: a battle was raging within his soul. Pharaoh thought of Dr. Breuerfliess and realized that he was far from cured, yet he could no longer bear his present state of vacillation.

At three in the morning, unable to sleep, mind stressed past all endurance, Pharaoh rose and began to pace back and forth in the garden. He roared like a lion. Birds woke and took refuge next door. To his horror he noticed that the limbs on a nearby tree were growing in straight lines. The only thing that saved him was that they were not at right angles to each other.

A laugh touched with dementia filled the night and he heard himself say, "A right curve!"

After pondering it awhile; Pharaoh came to the conclusion that the idea was far too depraved to be accepted by his contemporaries. Yet that was no reason to abandon it completely: he filed it away in that small corner of his brain where his most absurd notions were placed to germinate.

It was almost daybreak and Pharaoh suddenly realized he was hungry. While watching the brown rice simmer it came to him that he would have to leave this house. It had become a burden weighing heavily on the right side of his brain.

At the third spoonful of rice he recalled that it was time to order new supplies from the little gray man. A vision of the buxom beauties painted by Ingres came to him and he decided to name his next building The Turkish Bath. Contemporary architecture was so basely phallic: he was determined to construct a more feminine world. All he needed now was a sign, a wink from the gods.

Since Pharaoh adored the scent of night-blooming jasmine he always left the doors and windows open. He heard footsteps and it occurred to him that the Age of Corbusier, and his followers, was well over. The light, almost timid, footsteps drew nearer.

"This way," he said encouragingly. One never knew: it might even be Gaudi, in person. Pharaoh stood to greet his unexpected visitor.

Tense, watchful, one hand on the Welrod in her purse, Vida entered the room. She was clad in leather.

"I prayed the gods of shape and form to send me a sign, and here you are, the Goddess of Music, herself, the newest new face in the news."

Vida relaxed. All the Mafia bosses she had met lately were very classy guys.

"I would have called to say I was coming," she said, "but I have to be careful."

"Have you ever been here before?"

"Once, last year, for dinner with a friend from one of the New York families. He was here resting up after a heart attack. I did a little job for him."

"I've been worried about you. Were you badly hurt?"

"I'm healing. I was lucky: the knife didn't actually touch anything vital, but there was the possibility of peritonitis."

"You'll be safe here. You may stay as long as you like."

"Are you alone?"

"Yes."

"Thank you for your hospitality," said Vida.

"You must know how we all feel about you. You've become something of a celebrity. I'm sure things will work out."

"What I really need is to work," said Vida, sitting down next to Pharaoh.

"Are you well enough?"

"I don't need much money," she said. "It could even be an easy hit."

"Twenty thousand?"

"I must leave Los Angeles," said Vida. She thought it over. "All right, twenty thousand. Who..."

"I have to point them out to you," said Pharaoh. "Before we go I think you ought to change your appearance. You can't wander about the streets like that. A punk haircut dyed, oh, say, blue, would go nicely with your leather outfit. If you like, I'll help with the transformation. There's a supermarket on the other side of the house; I can buy whatever you need."

"With what family did you say you're connected?" asked Vida, amused by Pharaoh's unusual behavior.

"Las Vegas," said the greatest architect in the world, then, obeying an overwhelming, visceral impulse, he walked over to Vida and kissed her wildly in the absolute certainty that she could help abolish his rectitude.

"Let the tiger hunt begin," he muttered.

I Want My Champagne

HORACE PERCEVAL III READ Alba's question on his terminal then sent his limousine to pick her up. Gorodish was included in the dinner invitation.

Openmouthed with wonder, Alba and Gorodish stared out the window as the limousine drove through the gates and up past the pyramids.

"I feel like we're on a big pack of Camel's," said Alba.

"Magnificent," Gorodish said soberly.

Dressed in his usual uniform, Horace Perceval III came out of his pyramid just as the chauffeur opened the limo door.

"This is Serge Gorodish," said Alba. Gorodish bore down on the kid's fingers more than necessary, no doubt in reaction to an unconscious surge of jealousy.

"I'm in the middle of negotiations," said Horace Perceval III. "I'm trying to buy some of Vida's personal effects. The price is sure to go up."

"She is a fascinating creature," said Gorodish. "I have been collecting all the information I can about her."

"Come in," said Horace Perceval. Uncorking a bottle of Lanson champagne, he poured. "Do you work together?"

"No," said Gorodish, "we share a pagoda."

"Alba is brilliantly intuitive. I've sent out fifty people to check the houses my father either photographed or described. I've heard back from thirty-seven of them."

"Could your computer provide us with a dossier containing all available information on Vida?" said Gorodish.

"I'll ask B."

An hour later, a gorgeous morsel handed G a three-hundred-fifty-page printout. Alba glared at him: you can never tell what these depressive types might take it into their heads to do.

"I'm going for a walk," said Gorodish. Horace Perceval seemed so fascinated by Alba that Gorodish wanted to give her room to operate.

No sooner had he disappeared into the garden then Horace blushed, coughed to clear his throat and said, "I'll have a fortune when I retire, five years from now. I want to marry you."

"No way," said Alba. "I love Serge."

"What does he do?" asked Horace Perceval, struggling to regain his self-control.

"He plays."

"At what?"

"He plays with me, he plays the piano, he plays with money."

"People his age usually have atrophy of the brain."

"Not Serge," Alba said sharply.

"I beg your pardon."

Meanwhile, Gorodish was paying silent tribute to Pharaoh. As he approached one of the pyramids, Strawberry appeared. She was covered with paint. Pouting, she stared intently at Gorodish and said reproachfully, "You didn't bring your tools!"

"No," said Gorodish, taken aback.

"But on the telephone I told you I want to paint you with your jackhammer. Oh, well, take off your clothes so I can see if your body will do."

"Aren't we rushing things?" said Gorodish. "After all, I barely know you."

"Don't worry; everyone's a little shy at first. This is my fiftieth major canvas: I wouldn't want to work on a body that didn't inspire me."

"I don't think I'm the person you've been waiting for," said Gorodish. "I'm here visiting Horace Perce..."

"I was expecting a construction worker," said Strawberry. It sounded like an apology. "You seem a little young to have retired, but I expect hanging on to a jackhammer does age one. On the other hand, there *is* something rather interesting about you, a look ... too bad. Come to think of it, I might even have used you to end my Early Period."

"Perhaps we could work something out."

"What do you like best?"

"Music."

"Do you play?"

"The piano."

"Wonderful! I see you seated at a black Steinway, your nakedness contrasting with the black keys. The perfect apotheosis to my earliest works!"

"Come to dinner at our pagoda," said Gorodish. "We'll discuss it with Alba."

I Kissed Her Hard on the Lips

PHARAOH HANDLED SCISSORS the same way he did a pencil. Vida's hair looked like an old master drawing in which the discerning viewer might have noted primitive undulatory tendencies.

They were in the kitchen. Pharaoh had just applied the blue vegetable dye and, as a final touch, was covering Vida's eyelids with indigo shadow and silver glitter.

At that moment the little gray man walked in carrying a carton filled with brown rice, organic vegetables, carrot juice and a few exotic seasonings.

Vida recoiled.

"Sorry to bother you," said the little gray man, noticing the hair on the tile floor. Even before he recognized her there was a grin on his lips. This delivery was going to earn him a bigger tip than he had ever received. "I'll just charge it to your account," he said, and disappeared.

"Do you know him?" asked Vida.

"Of course."

"He's dangerous."

"That kind's too scared to..."

"You can never be too careful."

"Do you have, um, the tools of your trade with you?"

"In my bag."

"I think I'll buy a car," said Pharaoh. "What kind would you like?"

"A Porsche, with black-tinted windows," said Vida. This time it was she who impetuously kissed him.

Tristana Again

SINCE THE NAME OF VIDA'S fortune-teller was in the dossier, Gorodish decided to visit her. He immediately noticed the drooping bouquet of yellow tulips. Some of the petals had fallen.

Tristana glanced up from her newspaper. She looked exhausted, her face marked by the stress of answering cops' questions, reporters' questions, Cubans' questions. A machete lay next to her crystal ball.

"What's that for?" asked Gorodish. "You have to trepan your clients before you can read their minds?"

"First I read their minds, then I decide what to do about it."

"I'm no friend of Castro's."

"You don't look like the heat, and for sure you don't look like an investigative reporter. Let's see. I'll bet you have something to do with jazz."

"I try to, but I seem to be better at classical music."

"Let me see your hands," said Tristana. The machete was still within reach.

Gorodish sat down and held out his hands. Tristana examined them carefully. "I see frustrated talent, and a great love."

"How's my lifeline?"

"Long."

"My luck?"

"It's right here," said Tristana, digging her finger into Gorodish's tender palm. She examined the back of his hands, the shape of his fingers. "You're a very strange sort of artist: you're an idealist, but you like money."

"I can see that Vida knew what she was doing when she consulted you before killing those men. Were you able to foretell the problems she's having now?"

"Yes. I told her that Friday was a favorable day, but it turned out she had to work on a Saturday."

"She should have kept the Sabbath."

"Have you seen today's newspaper?"

"No."

Tristana handed him the paper she had been reading. Gorodish turned to the front page. A headline read:

JAZZ MUSICIANS TO GIVE TEN CONCERTS
HALF MILLION $ PROCEEDS TO GO TO
VIDA'S SAVIOR

"Interesting," said Gorodish.

"Did you notice the neon sign in my front window?"

"It isn't on."

"It burned out this morning."

"Will five hundred help fix it?"

"Five hundred? For that I'd predict the future for a whole five-man combo. We're talking serious business here. Wait a minute while I lock the front door."

Tristana concentrated. Gorodish tried to tell himself that not all palm readers were fakes. Somewhere in the history of fortune-telling there had to be three or four who were legitimate.

Tristana opened her eyes. She began to speak: "I see an Indigo Woman walking in the desert."

"A Taureg?"

"No, her skin is lighter. She walks through sand. Serpents glide about her feet but do not harm her. In the distance I can see a pyramid. It breathes, melts, billows, changes shape. Now it looks like the rocks you find at the water's edge. There are three tall towers, like those buildings downtown. In front of each tower is a dead man. The Indigo Woman is looking at another man. He seems to have come from the rock. His skin is golden and he looks like a king. I see him and the Indigo Woman in a large hall filled with women's bodies . . . they look like musical instruments. I hear songs. You're there, too. You speak to the Indigo Woman and the king, but they cannot hear you. They disappear. Now I see a black woman. Not an ordinary woman: a black virgin. The Indigo Woman tries to kill her, but the black virgin is indestructible. She speaks, and the Indigo Woman becomes her servant. The king is abandoned, alone. He builds a new palace. I hear more music. The black virgin is playing jazz. The jazz turns to gold. I can see it raining down on a Chinese pagoda. Inside the pagoda are two people who love each other."

Tristana wakened slowly as if coming out of a dream. Pensive, Gorodish handed her five hundred bucks. Back on the street again he felt as buoyant as a hot-air balloon.

Talented People Are Often Neurotic

THE BLACK PORSCHE WITH black-tinted windows pulled up in front of Tower Records on Sunset Strip, and Vida stepped out. Music was the one thing she had truly missed while on the run. Heading for the jazz section she bought thirty cassettes. Back in the Porsche, she slipped

Eric Dolphy and Ron Carter's "Magic" into the double-locked and armored Blaupunkt radio-cassette player.

Vida drove. The Porsche began to swing. In no time at all Vida was flying.

Pharaoh stared out at the passing buildings. A particularly ugly tower brought a flood of obscenities to his lips and he asked Vida to stop and back up. A brass plaque on one corner of the building identified the architect as one Norman Folkestone. Pharaoh glared at the tower as if readying himself to attack it with mace, broadsword and battering ram.

A chubby little man dressed like an artist and wearing glasses with yellow lenses came out of the building.

"That must be he," muttered Pharaoh,

The little man came nearer the Porsche. Pharaoh lowered the window and called, "Folkestone!"

Folkestone hesitated, his nostrils fluttering as he recognized Pharaoh. He smiled, lips stretched wide over yellow teeth. He looked like a banana *flambé* resting on a bed of strawberry ice cream and there was an expectant gleam in his eyes, as if he were the aforementioned dessert and a waiter had just poured the Grand Marnier and was about to light it.

"Why . . . you're Pharaoh . . . the Pharaoh, in person! I never thought I'd ever have the pleasure of . . ."

"What is this vertical pile of shit you're building?" screamed Pharaoh.

Folkestone blanched. He had noticed the Blue Angel who was about to lead him through the gates of hell.

"Will you do me the singular honor of putting a bullet through this wimp's head?" said Pharaoh, who had managed to regain control of himself.

A bullet whistled past Pharaoh's nose and buried itself in the architect's body. Folkestone went limp.

"I despise all discussion of aesthetics," said Pharaoh, in guise of a funeral oration.

"Hand me the Carla Bley tape," said Vida as she drove away. The car wound through Laurel Canyon. Vida smoked three cigarettes.

"What the hell were you doing in a Mafia safe house?" she asked.

"I was there by sheer chance," said Pharaoh. "I needed some time alone, by myself."

"I like you."

"Will you stay with me awhile?"

"Do you have any money?" asked Vida. "I could let you have the others at a discount."

"Done," said Pharaoh. "Are you hungry?"

"I know a good sushi bar in Venice."

"Let's go."

Carla Bley was cooking, Vida had found a kindred spirit and Pharaoh could feel an acute attack of sketchitis coming on. He was about to turn the world round.

* * *

Pharaoh's back teeth were swimming in sake; the fish had been so fresh he had almost felt the fins moving.

"How about two architects for dessert?" he asked.

"Which way are we going?"

"There is a hideous tower downtown. Its skin is made of absurd gold-colored mirrors and looks like a room in a French brothel built by someone who never did understand what the mirrors were for. The tower was designed by a nearsighted visionary who lives in a hanging garden overlooking the ocean at Santa Monica. The man is very organized. He regularly holds seminars and two floors of his house have been turned into dormitories for those who come to him thirsting for knowledge. At this very moment he is trying to convert a group of young Japanese architects to his foolishness."

Vida parked in front of the building. The sounds of a koto and *shakuhachi* could be heard, seemingly descending from the Immortals.

"We ought to bring him a present," said Pharaoh. "I noticed a Korean market on the corner: we'll find something there."

The outside elevator appeared to be lifting them directly toward Nirvana. The doors opened into what some might call a sumptuous apartment, its walls also covered with bronze-tinted glass. Pharaoh tried to hold back a grimace.

Sam Sunny Libchkowitz's party was winding down. The master of the house greeted them dressed in a simple dark kimono tied with a *heko-obi*.

"Pharaoh . . . you . . . here. I must call my guests back; they'll be so pleased. I think there's still a bottle of champagne. . . ."

"My assistant, Olga Vidalovitch."

"I didn't know you'd taken on an assistant. Have you changed your work habits?"

"Yes, I've become an advocate of expedience."

"No one can stand in the way of progress, Pharaoh."

Filling the center of the sitting room was a huge quadrilateral sculpture of polished bronze. It sparkled dazzlingly beneath a bright spotlight.

"What's that?" Pharaoh demanded.

"Oh, didn't you know? I've taken up sculpture," said Sam Sunny Libchkowitz with a fatuous smile.

"On your knees, you ignoramus!" Pharaoh thundered.

"What?" said Sam Sunny, collapsing onto the silvery carpet.

"Not only are you perverting the Japanese spirit but you are also an insult to these young architects' aesthetic sensibilities. You and your mirrors! You reflect only the hideous, the monstrous, the ugly. The Japanese have always venerated emptiness, space, the elliptical, the abstruse which, in leaving its mark on objects, reveals the infinite presence of Time. A patina, a shadow, is capable of provoking them to sensual heights you cannot even imagine. Your bronze cube, your mirrored buildings are an intolerable attack on all that the Japanese hold most dear!"

Pale and silent, Sam Sunny resignedly submitted to Pharaoh's verbal violence much as one waits for a drunken guest to leave one's home.

"All right," said Pharaoh after a brief silence, "so that you may atone for this affront I have brought you a brush and a can of black paint. You are going to paint your cube. I'm sure they will understand the message."

While Sam Sunny painted, Vida and Pharaoh drank a glass of champagne. "It's black, Pharaoh," Sam Sunny yelped, "it's black."

"Fine . . . the shape itself is disgusting but since we don't have a car crusher handy we'll forget that for the moment and go on . . . have you heard of Bushido?"

"Isn't that a new restaurant?"

"No; it's the samurai code of honor. Break the code of honor and there is only one thing left. . . ."

Vida pulled a Japanese sword from its black lacquered scabbard.

"A gift for you, Sunny," said Pharaoh.

"Are you going to kill me?"

"No; I am about to give you an opportunity to be reincarnated as, perhaps, someone with a little more taste. My assistant will instruct you in the proper manner of committing ritual suicide. Follow her directions exactly and you will die with dignity."

Vida held out the sword. To underline Pharaoh's words she also took out her Welrod.

The long ritual was scrupulously observed.

Around five in the morning the iniquitous architect's death rattle sounded, smothered within the shadowy sonorities of the *shakuhachi*.

Day broke as Vida and Pharaoh walked along Santa Monica Pier. Vida put her arm around Pharaoh affectionately.

"Why don't we have breakfast with the last architect?" he suggested. "I'll call him."

Vida was enjoying the quiet and the ocean air. She rather liked Pharaoh: there was something quite attractive about his implacable logic. She watched him walk back toward her, smiling.

"Wilter Bucket's going fishing," he said. "I told him to buy some croissants and pick us up here in his boat. The ocean is the perfect place to discuss a round world."

"Welcome aboard, Pharaoh. I've been wanting to meet you."

"I hope this white thing isn't a space shuttle."

"No, it's merely a fishing boat."

"This gentleman designs outer space ecologies," Pharaoh explained to Vida. "He's building the world of tomorrow: space here on earth, earth in space."

"Well, you've almost got it right," said Wilter Bucket. "Pharaoh is the greatest architect of the twentieth century; I am the greatest architect of the twenty-first."

"I'm so choked up I can barely swallow my croissant," said Vida.

Wilter Bucket was short and fat. A heavy black

beard and long hair gave him a passing resemblance to something out of a film by George Lukas.

The coffee was excellent, the croissants airy. Soon they were in null-G, tacking toward Point L5 between earth and the moon.

"To what do I owe the long-deferred honor of your visit?" asked Wilter Bucket, brushing away the croissant crumbs dotting his beard.

"I want us to have a drawing contest," Pharaoh said distractedly.

"What a curious idea. We should have alerted the media for an event of this magnitude. I always have a sketchpad and pencils with me, you know how it is. . . . Genius is often a true burden to carry."

"True," said Pharaoh. "Now, for the rules: we will each do a drawing. There must be no straight lines. My assistant will act as judge and her decision is final. When we are finished we will hand her our sketches. She will study them and shoot the loser."

"I like your gallows humor, Pharaoh. Shall we begin?"

Twenty minutes later they were finished. Pharaoh had drawn a woman, Wilter Bucket, circles. Unfortunately he had signed his work.

Wilter Bucket slipped overboard, a bullet in his heart.

"How did you know he'd sign his name?" asked Vida.

"He's the sort that would give a bum his autograph instead of a handout."

I Am Dirty

ONE CUBAN WITH A TATTOO on his hand, hanging around all day reading a newspaper, is curious. A second Cuban, sitting in a car a hundred feet away, might be a coincidence. But when the shoeshine boy is chewing on a fifteen-dollar Havana cigar it's time to pack up and head for home so as not to wind up as another innocent passerby wounded, and especially if one is the very embodiment of the architecture of the future.

They were about to turn into the driveway of Pharaoh's rented house when Vida, who had seen a lot of Westerns, decided that the street was too quiet. She kept driving, waiting for a truck to swerve into their path, for a palm tree to fall in front of the Porsche, for a fake cop to fire at them. To her surprise nothing happened.

"Did you forget something, darling?" asked Pharaoh.

"Who'll design my mausoleum if you're not around to do it?"

"Jazz will."

"I forgot to pick up some Havana cigars."

"Do you smoke cigars?"

"No, but the whole neighborhood reeks of them: nine-mm cigars, thirty-aught-six cigars. I don't know: maybe we ought to call for some Vietnamese backup. Hold on to your seat; let's see what this baby can do."

She downshifted into second just as Charlie Parker began to wail, laying down a series of time changes that had absolutely nothing in common with what you get from a metronome. Vida followed his chameleon rhythms and the Cubans, who danced to a more languorous beat, were left behind. Just as the Charlie Parker number ended Vida pulled up to a telephone booth.

"Skip, it's Vida."

"Why haven't you telephoned?"

"I didn't have a minute to myself."

"How can I help?"

"I can give you the Cubans, but I'll need you to carry out a, um, preemptive strike."

Vida explained. Amazed, Skip informed the Vietnamese. The Mafia safe house was about to become a killing ground.

Meanwhile, Vida and Pharaoh decided to risk being recognized and went to hear McCoy Tyner, who was appearing at "Concerts by the Sea."

Cuban Cigars
Are Murder

NOTHING RESEMBLES A JUNgle so much as a neglected garden at night. The Cubans, who had waited all day for Vida to show up, had no idea that a troop of almost invisible Vietnamese was now crawling toward them through the underbrush.

Encino is not Chicago in the thirties: anyone living in the house could have been sitting on the patio, reading a book, and not known that death was in the air.

The Vietnamese considered the Mafia's request a strange one but attributed its extravagance to an overworked imagination and a culture influenced by grand opera. Still, they carried out the action with scrupulous attention to detail and with as much care as if they had been asked to prepare a dish of *Pha go* garnished with transistors.

Boys and Girls

HORACE PERCEVAL III'S employees traveled by bicycle, and it took them awhile, but a colony of ants working steadily can often move more earth than a tornado. The kids searched the gardens and mansions on the list and infiltrated themselves everywhere. Even guard dogs hesitated to attack them: there was so little to chew on.

At last, part of the armada reached the Mafia safe house. Having been raised on the classics, the group's female mascot said, "Something's wrong. It's too quiet. I'll ring the doorbell and say I'm collecting for the Motion Picture Academy Home."

Silently as Sioux, the others spread out and hid. The front door was open; the little girl entered and immediately found those Pharaonic traces Horace had told them to watch for: a first edition of *The Long Goodbye* and a sketchpad filled with drawings.

Picking up the telephone, she reported her find and included such other details as blue vegetable dye and hair on the kitchen floor. While talking, she tried to imagine Pharaoh blued.

Leaving the house, she found the other members of the search party bending over a good number of dead Cubans. The bodies lay half-hidden in the tall grass and all appeared to have choked to death on submarine-sized cigars that had been jammed down their throats. The children could just make out the gold-printed red bands behind gold- and silver-filled teeth.

"Fidel Castro did it," said one of the kids.

"No, it was the CIA," said the little girl, who knew what she was talking about.

Returning to the house they telephoned Horace Perceval III. He, in turn, asked counsel of his guru, Baba Ramesh Baba, Esq., then, unsatisfied, decided that Gorodish could give him more practical advice.

When not negotiating business deals Horace Perceval III had problems dealing with reality.

"Serge, it's Horace Perce..."

"Alba's at her office."

"I need your advice. We've found the house where my father's been hiding."

"Alba will be delighted to hear it."

"But my father is no longer there, and there are twenty-three dead Cubans in the garden, all of whom appear to have choked to death on their cigars."

"Buy up the cigars, if the ends haven't been bitten off."

"My guru says, 'There is no smoke without fire.'"

"Spiritually correct. Pick me up; I'll take a look."

Some Crazy Stuff

Fingers aching from five continuous hours of practice, Gorodish finished playing the latest addition to his repertoire (*Bagatelles*, opus 126, by Ludwig von Beethoven) then sat back and tried to hold very still, as a good model should. He was naked.

Strawberry was putting the finishing touches to her masterpiece while Alba made spaghetti sauce. The odor of garlic, basil and olive oil teased Gorodish's nostrils. At that moment a detail from Tristana's prediction skittered across his mind, moving as quickly as a thirty-second note.

"Are you almost finished?" he asked Strawberry.

"I have to do the highlight in the eye. The eyes are very important, like when you're buying fish."

"Thanks for the comparison."

Alba gazed admiringly at the painting of Gorodish nude. "Beautiful," she said. "Just think, one day you'll be hanging in a museum, or be on the back of a book jacket."

"I do believe it's the best work I've ever done," said Strawberry. "I hope my father can be there for the opening of my exhibition."

"You'll have the kid before that happens," said Gorodish.

"This business about the Cubans has stirred up a hornets' nest. Everyone's talking about it. Let's hope they never realize my father's involved."

"Don't worry," said Gorodish, "I made sure the house is clean."

"Pearl O'Pearl's furious. Tomorrow night the Los Angeles Philharmonic will premier her *Orpheus* but it won't be the same if Pharaoh isn't there to hear it."

Gorodish dressed, his brain churning like a food processor.

"Are seats still available?"

"At a price."

"Then Pharaoh will be there."

"How do you know?" asked Alba.

"I read it in the clouds of smoke from Cuban cigars."

Strawberry packed up her paints but left the canvas, which needed time to dry. Gorodish slurped down spaghetti and stared out at the ocean.

"Want to hear a scoop?" he asked.

"What?" said Alba.

"Pharaoh's not the one with the blue hair. It's Vida. They're together. She killed those three architects as a favor to Pharaoh."

"I said the same thing to Horace Perceval not three hours ago," said Alba. "Anything else?"

"Yes. The black virgin will change everything."

"Who?" demanded Alba. "You mean to say there are other virgins around here besides me?"

"Yes. And the pagoda will be covered with a shower of gold."

"Posing nude has gone to your head," said Alba. "You're acting strange, weird, bizarre."

"The king," said Gorodish. "And the Indigo Woman."

"Horace Perceval's mother is a well-known psychoanalyst. Maybe she'll only charge you whole-sale."

"Let's go to bed," said Gorodish; "I'll tell you the story of Orpheus, so you'll know what's going on tomorrow night."

Nuts

THEY WERE LATE: PEARL O'Pearl's *Orpheus* was scheduled to start in twenty minutes. The Cadillac raced down the freeway toward the Music Center, Gorodish torn between watching the road and watching Alba. She had outdone herself this evening and was wearing a black leotard and dance tights, a length of transparent pink garden hose braided through her hair, looped around her throat and spiraling down her torso, its free end dangling next to her left leg. Inside the pink tube were tiny Japanese Christmas-tree lights that blinked on and off and served to heighten the darkly sculpted, Brancusilike effect of Alba's body.

In contrast, Gorodish was a study in classicism: shoes, trousers, a shirt, tie and jacket.

Out of breath, they reached the best seats the last row of the orchestra had to offer. For the moment the audience was the show, the flower of Los Angeles society whipping itself into a frenzy as some idiot woman tried to bring a lion into the auditorium under the pretext that her pet loved music.

Also in attendance were studio execs, past, present and future stars, painters, musicians, cackling parrots disguised as women, and critics from New

York, Boston and Chicago, not to mention the local press.

The concert had been sold out for six weeks. Scalpers were asking, and getting, five hundred dollars a ticket.

Gorodish did not waste his time on anthropological observation. Somewhere in the crowd was a head of blue hair and a Pharaoh.

The composer entered. Melomaniacs in the audience commented on her appearance. She looked bleached out, lips blue, eyelids as pale and swollen as a hack writer's metaphor.

The critics began taking notes. The orchestra had been reorganized along strangely classical lines, its various sections arranged as if to play Mahler. There was even a podium for the conductor. Was the enfant terrible of minimalist music *that* intimidated by the reputation of the orchestra about to play her work?

The violins entered with their violins, the violas with their violas, the celli ditti. The double basses were already onstage so that was that.

It was only when the woodwinds appeared that things became interesting. Thirty nurses entered, pushing wheelchairs. Each chair held a sort of plastic bellows that was connected to the woodwind's mouthpiece, the instruments' keys blocked so that each could play only a single note. As for the percussionists, they were as human as any orchestra musician can be.

Instead of pushing the usual grand piano into

place, stagehands now rolled out a small glass tank. Orpheus and Eurydice entered, stage left, and climbed into it. They were naked. Thunderous applause.

The program notes reminded the audience that the librettist of the work they were about to hear was Horatio Glockenspiel, a young poet famous among the local avant-garde for the innovative quality of his hallucinatory imagery. Originally the text was to have been recited by a computer-generated voice housed in a robot, its space-opera appearance intended to conjure up images of the hero as a synthesis of twentieth-century mythology. However the composer, desiring to retain the musicality of the Italian in which the text was written, had decided to assign the major portion of the narrative to a mynah bird. The machine stood onstage now, holding a small gold cage containing the bird. Technicians bustled about, adjusting microphones.

The house lights dimmed. Whistles, shouts, applause. A blue-white spot lit one corner of the stage. The only thing missing now was the conductor.

Two stagehands tied a cluster of bananas to the railing around the conductor's podium. Economy of gesture is no longer admired in the concert trade, and the new school of conductors tends to the Olympic, rather than the Olympian, certain of them being so exuberant that they have been known to nail one shoe to the floor to keep from falling.

The conductor entered. He was a baboon. Dressed in tails, he toddled through the massed musicians with great dignity.

Whispers could now be heard from the audience as the season subscribers commented on his achievements. Even as an infant he had loved music. One day a guard at the zoo noticed that Mozart brought tears to his eyes; soon after he was enrolled in a conservatory where he specialized in music of the baroque period. According to several of the world's most influential critics, he brought to his interpretations an incomparable intelligence and an acute, even though revisionist, sensitivity. His bio also noted that it was the French who had first recognized his genius, awarding him a gold medal for his album and praising his handsome, nay, noble appearance when compared to certain other well-known, human conductors. In short, the baboon's prestige well matched the importance of tonight's occasion. This was his American debut.

The baboon climbed onto the podium in the usual fashion, holding on to the bar as he bowed to the audience. Then, with an imperious look in his eye, he turned to the orchestra. The musicians waited tensely for the upbeat. With a grand, absolutely professional sweep of his arm, the concert began.

His conducting style was amazingly precise. Plastic bellows produced their several single notes; Orpheus and Eurydice blew bubbles underwater, the sound amplified just enough to be heard. The robot announced the beginning of each movement and sequence and summarized the plot in fine, Brechtian style, while the mynah, in splendid voice, recited Horatio Glockenspiel's text. In order to assure the absolute randomness demanded by the score from time to time the baboon plucked a banana from the bunch hanging behind him and threw it to the orchestra. Following the directions in the score, the musician who caught it put down his instrument, ate the banana, then began playing again where he had left off. Thus (as the critics pointed out) the act of throwing a banana introduced the factor of chance into the performance and led to a Homeric struggle between the human element of the orchestra and the transcendent, disincarnate continuity of sound coming from the bellows-equipped woodwinds. In other words, Pearl O'Pearl had just invented metaphysical minimalism.

The audience, social philharmonists and music lovers alike, were agreed that the baboon was a genius. Only the ever-vigilant critic from the *Los Angeles Times* noticed (with his Oxford-trained eye) that in the fifty-third measure after the letter D the conductor had misread the score and eaten a banana which the composer had not intended. The article ended with the critic passing off this small blunder as forgivable, if not forgettable, and indicating that, in his opinion, no conductor since Toscanini had displayed so fiery a sense of tempo.

The naked swimmers shocked no one except a

Swiss critic. The majority of the audience was of the opinion that Pearl O'Pearl's score did, indeed, distill the mythological quintessence of the narrative, and said so.

Only Horatio Glockenspiel was unhappy: seven minutes into the first movement the mynah had come to a phrase he found particularly pleasing and had stuck there, repeating it over and over.

One last toss of a banana and *Orpheus* was part of musical history. The composer came onstage, congratulated the orchestra and soloists, shook hands with the conductor and bowed to the audience. Applause, shouts, whistles. To close the concert the composer made a brief curtain speech: "Never again will a banana be thought of as merely a banana!"

More applause. Next day her words were reprinted in the nation's newspapers.

Horace Perceval III rounded out his evening by buying two or three baubles to resell at a profit if the evening ever came to be thought of as an event of historical importance.

Strawberry stared at Alba's blinking lights. Pearl O'Pearl signed a contract with the manager of the Bolshoi Theater who saw, in the use of a baboon as conductor of a major symphony orchestra, signs of an anti-imperialist statement.

Pharaoh had been meditating on the shapes of the instruments and so had not heard the music. Vida had been dreaming about jazz. Pulling the plugs from his ears Gorodish plunged through the crowd after Pharaoh and Vida, who were taking French leave. He would catch up with Alba later, at the pyramids.

Nobody Fools with Me

GORODISH'S PLAN HAD BEEN concocted during one long, sleepless night. His scheme was not entirely rational, in fact it was somewhat surrealistic, but when dealing with an exceptional being one tailors one's tactics accordingly. He had brought fifteen thousand dollars with him to the concert, the money intended as the down payment on a contract with Vida. If his plan worked, Gorodish would retrieve the money; if he was lucky, a magnanimous heaven would return it to him multiplied. In either case he would have the satisfaction of having saved jazz by saving Vida.

Pushing past a pair of bejeweled scarecrows Gorodish hurried after Pharaoh and Vida who were heading for the exit. They looked not exactly worried, merely a little tense. So what if the Cubans had been cigared? The police were still after them. Vida's purse looked heavy, and strangely misshapen. No doubt that faithful servant, Sir Welrod, was napping inside, a bullet resting peacefully beneath his firing pin. Gorodish hoped Vida would not mistake him for a cop.

His telephone number was on the money envelope, in the event Vida needed further instructions, or more cash. He tried to think of a way to make her notice him, a way to give her the envelope without attracting undue attention. Her car was probably parked in the underground garage. Gorodish took the elevator even though he knew there was no way he could follow their car. This was not the movies.

Vida whispered something to Pharaoh, then went into the ladies' room. Gorodish hung back, reluctant to follow her for fear a horde of enraged females might throw him out. But it takes people a few seconds to react to the unexpected, and he could always claim that Pearl O'Pearl's music had befuddled his mind.

Gorodish pushed his way into the rest room. A woman was rinsing her eyeglasses, another was powdering her nose. He didn't even have to jump up and down to spot a tuft of blue hair, for only one stall was occupied. Taking the envelope from his pocket he quickly slid it under the stall door. A pair of eyes began to widen. A mouth began to form an O of indignation. He left the rest room.

Gorodish moved upstream through the crowd. Pharaoh paid no attention to him but stood, absorbed in some inner vision of his own, looking like a figure in a Goya painting.

Vida came out of the ladies' room, one hand in

her purse, eyes sweeping the crowd. Gorodish ostentatiously looked the other way. Vida grabbed Pharaoh and pulled him toward the Porsche.

She did not relax again until after a long, viciously complicated and dangerous series of turns and back-tracking designed to lose any cars that might be following.

"What's going on?" Pharaoh asked worriedly.

"Nothing. While I was in there, pissing, someone slipped me fifteen thousand dollars."

"The price of fame. Where are we going to sleep tonight?"

"We'll take a bungalow at the Tropicana Motel."

"Do you think the police will ever learn who leased the house in Encino?"

"The Mafia is so open and aboveboard," said Vida. "They just love talking to the cops. Did you pay by check?"

"Cash."

"Then the only one who might have a problem is the guy who brought you the Malevich."

Nice Work

IT WAS ALMOST DAWN WHEN Strawberry and her friends brought Alba home. She had begun to feel strange emotions every time Strawberry held and kissed her: she wanted to stay in the other girl's arms.

Slipping off her shoes, Alba walked toward the beautiful glimmer of the ocean. Sunrise. Alba removed her tube and entered the water, imagining it was Strawberry.

Dripping, she returned to the pagoda and found Gorodish surrounded by tools and electronic brica-brac.

"Turning your Steinway into a synthesizer, darling?"

"You don't often call me 'darling.'"

"Would it shock you if I said I'm a little bit in love with Strawberry?"

"Bring me a Valium and a large glass of iced tea. This last spot is a hard one to solder."

Alba returned a few minutes later, dry, clothes changed, carrying tea and the small blue pill. Gorodish looked pleased with himself.

"What are you doing to that tape recorder?"

"Merely rewiring it a little. I need you to record something for me. The test is on the piano."

"Alba read the script and burst out laughing. "Are you sure you're feeling all right, Serge?"

"Marvelous. I just need some sleep, that's all."

"You want me to record this now?"

"Yes. The phone may ring at any moment and I'll have to go out. Try to read it as sweetly as you can."

Gorodish lay down and listened to his angel's beautiful voice perfectly portraying a virgin. He was about to slip deep into an abyss of blue marshmallows when he felt Alba's body next to his. Taking him in her arms she whispered softly to him until he fell asleep. Her beach-bum Rachmaninoff was having a hard time of it; she would have to start taking better care of him. A strong man who cracks can collapse faster than a skyscraper in the hands of the Stefanelli Brothers, Demolitions.

Turn Blue

WHEN GORODISH WOKE HE was still in his nymph's arms and his brain was functioning again. As he crawled from the bed Alba stretched and murmured something. Gorodish turned away, headed directly for the Guatemala

Antigua and brewed a pint of joe. After a five-minute shiver under the cold shower, he draped himself in a bath towel and sat down at the piano to think. Alba sleepwalked across the room and sat down beside him. Her body smelled of the sea, its undercurrents helping orchestrate Gorodish's thoughts.

Sparkling light filled the pagoda. Alba took three sips from Gorodish's cup, kissed his neck and said, "Want to play a duet?"

"It's time you started taking your piano practice seriously."

"I will, after I find Pharaoh. With the money I'm going to make I'll be able to hire anyone I want to give me lessons."

"Not just anybody," Gorodish warned. "There's nothing better than the Russian technique."

"Okay, whatever you say. But right now I'm worried about Pharaoh."

Gorodish struck a series of chords. "Telephone Horace Perceval and have him get the money ready: Papa-Pharaoh will soon be back in Pyramid City."

"Has all that Valium you've been taking made you clairvoyant?"

"No; it was Tristana."

"Who?"

"A friend of Vida's. She tells fortunes in the form of parables. So far, everything she predicted has come true."

"I don't understand how a professional killer can be superstitious."

"I can. I'm trying to make things move along a little faster."

"Do you guarantee that Pharaoh will be home soon?"

"It's written in the stars."

Gorodish dressed, picked up his electronic gizmos and climbed into the Cadillac, which had been baking in the sun.

Taking the freeway he headed back downtown and spent the next hour driving up and down the streets in the Chicano neighborhoods of East Los Angeles, visiting more churches than he had in his preceding fifty lifetimes. He was almost at the end of his patience when he pushed open one last termite-ridden door and found himself in a pink stucco sanctuary. The place looked like it belonged in a Western; the effect was overwhelming: it was exactly what he had been looking for. A priest with a Sal Mineo face walked toward him, rubbing his hands.

"How's business?" asked Gorodish, almost crushing the padre's damp fingers.

"That's the first time I've heard it put quite that way."

"I'm not surprised," said Gorodish. "People are so materialistic, they never spare a thought for the men doing God's work. But I do."

"How thoughtful of you. Are you new in the neighborhood?"

"I was just passing through when I suddenly felt an overwhelming need to commune with God."

"When was your last confession?"

"My behavior being predicated on an extremely strict set of moral values, I cannot recall having sinned lately. The problem is that I am rather neurotic and need absolute quiet in order to pray. Therefore, I am about to do a good deed."

Taking one thousand dollars from his pocket, Gorodish handed the money to the priest who looked as if, maybe, his prayers had been answered after all. "God has sent you," he stammered.

"He's so busy," said Gorodish, "that sometimes he has to delegate authority. You are to give me the keys to the church and leave me alone until tomorrow. I'll leave the keys in the lock when I go."

Smiling blissfully, the good Father tossed Gorodish the keys, and vanished. Gorodish carried in his gadgets and locked the door.

Two hours later, sanctified by his work, he returned to the pagoda.

"Some chick telephoned," said Alba. "She didn't leave her name but she'll call back tonight."

"That was Vida."

"Are you sure you haven't been taking too many tranquilizers?"

"We have just enough time for dinner. I'm starving."

"Me, too. Where are you going to take me?"

"To an Italian restaurant. I want to establish an atmosphere."

"What sort of atmosphere?"

"Of mysticism."

"This is starting to feel like a misological mystic miscalculation."

Gorodish ordered pasta Alfredo, a bottle of Lacrima Christi, and antipasto for Alba who, despite her Italian origins, had never gotten the hang of the Holy Mysteries.

It's a Wonder You Can Stay Alive

PHARAOH WAS AWAKENED BY a furious need to scribble and hurried out to buy a sketchpad and pencil. There was a coffeepot in the bungalow. While Vida ate the French toast ordered in from a nearby café, Pharaoh began blackening blank pages.

"What are those limp bubbles you're drawing?" she asked.

Pharaoh picked at his sugar-coated toast and kept on sketching. When he was working there was about as much chance of getting an answer from him as from the moon.

Vida cleaned her Welrod, handling it with the care one might give a Stradivarius. At nine in the evening she telephoned her mysterious new employer.

"This is Vida."

"I'm glad you decided to call. I was afraid you might turn me down. I am one of your most fervent admirers, and I was hoping, in the name of music, that there was some way I could help."

The voice was so sugary, the words so honeyed, that Vida felt as if she might become stuck in them. "Nobody helps nobody with nothing," she said. "I do the job, you pay me, and that's it."

"True, yet there are certain aspects of this. . . ."

"Where, when, who, how much?"

"I've paid you the first half. Tonight, the church at 1042 Chiltepiquin Street. The target will be alone there, praying. She'll be facing you. I want her out of my life forever. The rest of the money is under the last pew in the back row, to the left. I know this may sound strange, but I beg you to show no mercy. Oh, I almost forgot: there's a pine tree near the front door of the church. You'll find the key buried at the foot of it. You can leave the key in the lock when you're finished. I trust I may count on you?"

"It's as good as done," said Vida and hung up.

Pharaoh stretched and sipped at his coffee. "Aren't you worried it might be a trap?"

"If this nut wanted to kill me he could have done it last night instead of giving me an envelope full of money."

"I'll be waiting." Pharaoh stood in the doorway and watched the Porsche disappear into the night.

Vida parked down the street from the church. She was calm, but could feel herself borne along by strange sensations. For the first time in her life she no longer felt in control of her actions, no longer the leading actor in her own story: it was as if she were merely a spectator on the sidelines, as if she were suddenly in the hands of fate.

No one was watching her; she could feel nothing wrong about the street, or the people passing by. She walked toward the church, making no effort to appear inconspicuous, no effort to hide. Five young Chicanos sat on the hood of a low-rider, talking loudly. Their voices did not slow as Vida passed them. She took a deep breath. The air was filled with the scent of frangipani.

Finding the key she entered the church and stood just inside the door more than a minute, trying to make her mind a blank, trying to look as if she had entered on impulse. The church was empty. Vida took the Welrod from her purse and waited. More than an hour went by before it occurred to her to see if the other half of her fee was where it was supposed to be. The man had kept his word. To pass the time she counted the money.

Only the nave and altar were lit. Vida felt dislocated, as if she were somehow outside of time. It was not an unpleasant sensation. Little by little she felt a radiance growing within her, dispelling her anguish. Outside, the streets were silent. Vida could feel the weight of that silence.

An incredibly beautiful wood polychrome statue of a black Virgin stood at the altar. Vida studied the Virgin's face. Minutes passed. The statue seemed to move slightly, a small smile, a quirking of the fine brows.

Suddenly she realized what her client wanted of her: she was to kill the black Virgin. He had to be a madman, or a fetishist.

Slowly, Vida raised the Welrod and took aim at the Virgin's heart. Even with the silencer the shot was almost deafening. The statue must have been solidly bolted to the altar, for it did not fall when the bullet penetrated the Virgin's heart. Vida put the Welrod back in her purse and was turning to leave when the Virgin said:

"Don't go, Vida. From this day forward you are mine. You must come to me. You cannot escape your destiny. I shall save you. Take refuge in me. If your faith is pure and true the world will have no power over you and you will be safe, untouchable, within the communion of souls."

Two tears slid down Vida's face as she stood motionless before the black Virgin.

To Say Goodbye Is to Die a Little

IT WAS ONLY WHEN THE delivery man handed Pharaoh the check that he realized he had eaten twelve pizzas and drunk five quarts of Coca-Cola. And he must have napped occasionally, for the plans of his first project absolutely devoid of straight lines were finished.

"Vida?"

There was no answer. Pharaoh tried to remember something of his last three days of creative delirium; Vida's image did not appear in any of his memories. He brewed a pot of coffee. Obviously, she had abandoned him and had probably taken the Porsche across the border into Mexico. Pharaoh rolled up his sketches, paid the motel manager, listening distractedly as she told him how a piece of someone's nose had been found in the ice machine, then walked down the hill to Santa Monica Boulevard.

The sky was still deep blue and there was still a black Porsche in the parking lot. Pharaoh approached it hesitantly. The keys were under the floor mat and there was an envelope on the driver's seat. He turned on the air conditioning.

Pharaoh,
  I have gone to seek my destiny. You will never see me again. Don't worry; I am more alive now than I have ever been.

Vida

He shook his head. Vida had shot through his life like a comet, had helped him give birth to a new style. He would always be grateful to her.

Pharaoh drove to the office of the largest building contractor in Los Angeles and spent five hours discussing materials, engineering details and completion dates. When everything was settled, he headed back to Pyramid City and brought the car skidding to a stop in front of Dr. Breuerfliess's house. The good doctor could not hide her joy at seeing her patient cured.

"You're looking wonderful, Tut," she said, "full of vigor and energy, and your eyes are shining."

"Move everything out of your pyramid and into the garden."

"What's going on? Is there going to be an earthquake?"

"Better than that."

Climbing back into the Porsche, Pharaoh drove to Suzy's house, where he found her making love to her latest student who, having heard tales of Pharaoh's legendary tolerance in such matters, stood to meet him, penis high, a smile on his lips, one hand outstretched in greeting. Pharaoh broke a Chinese ceramic urn over his head. The student collapsed. Since he wasn't dead, Pharaoh said, "Get out of here or I'll kill you."

Suzy began to cry.

"If there's anything you really want to keep, you'd better move it out of the pyramid *now*."

"You've gone crazy!"

"Quite the contrary; I'm completely cured."

The Porsche's engine almost blew a valve head as Pharaoh zoomed up to Pearl O'Pearl's pyramid where he repeated his orders before going on to Strawberry's studio. He found her necking with Alba.

"Making a baby?" he asked sarcastically.

"You're back! How wonderful!"

"Move your daubs and smears out of here if you hope to save them."

Horace Perceval III was in the process of selling Clark Gable's yacht to an Italian count.

"Hi, Papa; I missed you. I've been waiting for you to come home."

"Unplug those damn computers and move them out of here. There're going to be some changes made."

"What do you mean?"

At that moment there came a deafening noise: it sounded as if Russian tanks had invaded Pyramid City. Women screamed. Horace Perceval III came running out of his pyramid and discovered, to his horror, ten bulldozers moving into position around the edge of the property.

"You're freaking out!" All he got for his trouble was a slap.

In a panic Suzy, Kim and the girls descended on Pharaoh, who remained calm and in control of the situation.

Quickly gathering his wits Horace Perceval III said, "You're not actually going to tear down this masterpiece of American architecture, are you? I'll buy the pyramids from you. I'll have them dismantled and moved somewhere else. I can sell them to someone. . . ."

Pharaoh was too busy defending himself against his wives and daughters to respond to the offer: someone had managed to claw his face.

Bloody, but still on his feet, Pharaoh let loose a cry that frightened the birds from the trees: "Enough!"

"You're crazy, tearing down the pyramids, historic monuments, national treasure...."

"I'm going to build you a paradise," said Pharaoh. "All you have to do is be patient for a few weeks. I can't stand the sight of straight lines anymore, and I will not allow this example of my early work to remain standing!"

"But there are photographs of the pyramids everywhere," said Horace. "And there's all your earlier work, too. Destroying the pyramids is as evil an act as was the burning of the library at Alexandria."

Pharaoh ignored him. Pearl O'Pearl was in hysterics. Suzy was sitting in the grass, sniffling. Dr. Breuerfliess was chanting incantations to the spirit of Lacan. Strawberry renewed her attack on her father, who punched her in the eye.

"Where will we live?" Horace Perceval III asked resignedly.

"I've ordered a geodesic dome," said Pharaoh. "We'll all live there together until the new buildings are finished."

"Can't we have him declared incompetent and committed to a state hospital?" Suzy asked Dr. Breuerfliess.

"It's against my principles. Anyway, in my opinion, he's completely sane. Perhaps too sane. Now we're the ones in trouble."

Pharaoh's little family fluttered off, like a flock

of sparrows trying to save a part of their nests.

Alba, who had been watching the scene with great interest, walked beside Pharaoh as he moved toward the bulldozers. She even took his hand.

"You got some balls," she said.

"Thank you."

"I'm Alba."

"Delighted to meet you."

"Serge likes you."

"Who's Serge?"

"He's my friend," said Alba. "I'm not really a lesbian, you know. What you saw was merely a momentary excess of affection."

"I've got nothing against lesbianism," said Pharaoh.

"Really?"

"Quite the contrary: it fits perfectly with the work I'm going to be doing from now on."

"How's that?" asked a stunned Alba.

"There's no rigidity in lesbianism, no straight lines. If I seemed unhappy about my wife's lover, it was strictly from an aesthetic point of view. That thing sticking up in the air was an affront to my sensibilities."

"I understand," said Alba.

An hour later the pyramids were gone, having disappeared in a cloud of dust and noise. That same night the family gathered under the dome. Pharaoh sat up until dawn, explaining to an awestruck Gorodish his plans for Sinuo City.

Sinuo City

WITH HORACE PERCEVAL III fulfilling his part of the bargain, and with what Alba had accomplished, it was obvious that Pink & Pink would soon have a long list of distinguished clients. Since Pharaoh was allowing no one outside the immediate family onto the construction site, Alba invited Strawberry and Gorodish to accompany her to Baja California for a short rest.

There, they found a Van Ness so ecstatically happy that he even seemed to have forgotten he had once been a detective. Whether it was the workings of his imagination, or the effects of the tequila, he now firmly believed that his entire life had been spent deep-sea fishing, and had even invented a complex and detailed personal history in support of his new memories. He had also become something of a local hero.

What with the beach, boat rides, exotic liquors and excursions into the interminable hot nights which caused torpid bodies to ride to Ellingtonian heights of ecstasy, weeks passed.

Then one morning, a telegram arrived. Sinuo City was ready; one thousand A-list guests had been asked to the opening.

Even the Cadillac acted as if it had been on a tequila bender: jovial, giddy on the straightways, it sometimes almost managed to forget its age.

A lighthearted Gorodish drove, while in the backseat Alba and Strawberry swapped spit and stories, revealed secrets, made promises. Gorodish watched their copper-toned bodies and the ocean, and thought about Vida. She had disappeared. The press had grown bored with the story and were now talking about a sadist who had taken to raping and strangling one or two women a week. Vida had become a myth, her image purified. Gorodish had almost begun to doubt her existence. Perhaps he had fantasized her, or seen her in a hallucination.

The trip back to Los Angeles was slow, hot and difficult; they were going to be late. Strawberry had forgiven Pharaoh and now could not wait to see his new work. She was returning to Los Angeles with seven sketchpads filled with drawings of their vacation. After so many months spent painting old people she now planned to paint nothing but Alba and could already visualize an impressive array of canvases, the next period in her life and work.

Leaving the freeway, Gorodish took the coast road, drove past Marina del Rey and Venice, headed up the Pacific Coast Highway below the Palisades, and turned up Sunset Boulevard. They followed its meanderings, the best possible prelude to what awaited them deep in the jungles of Bel-Air.

About a half mile from Pharaoh's property they found themselves at the tail end of a long line of cars. Abandoning the Cadillac, they covered the rest of the way on foot. Photographers scurried about. Cameras clicked.

At the gate, some nasty-looking muscle was checking invitations. A tarpaulin had been draped over the fence around the property so that Pharaoh's creation would not be seen by the uninvited. A helicopter filled with free-lance reporters flew overhead.

Gorodish pushed his way through. Their names were on the list. They walked through the gate, took a few steps and stopped, stunned.

An artificial stream now ran from the property's highest point, cascading downward and branching into small ponds, its width varying from thirty to ninety feet. Where the pyramids had once stood there were now huge, smooth black boulders of varying shapes. The boulders, which were made of glass and resembled the tide-polished rocks found at the water's edge, reflected the trees and new flowering plants. One of the rocks lay half-submerged in a pond, only its top visible. Strawberry was seized by such a frenzy of artistic emotion that she collapsed, weeping, in Alba's arms. Alba's throat was tight. Gorodish was not in much better shape.

After a moment, Alba said, "It's the Tao."

Round tables dotted the grounds. Horace Perceval III's hand could be seen in the buffet which was comprised of dishes, accompanied by their chefs, from all over the world. The guests were in raptures.

The trio set off in search of Pharaoh, Kim, Suzy, Pearl O'Pearl and Horace Perceval III.

Inside the first of the black structures they came upon Dr. Kim Breuerfliess who, surrounded by the cream of American psychoanalysis, was watching and listening while several of her patients floated in a zero-G bubble.

There seemed to be no angles within the black boulder, light entered the structure at random and the nearby water reflected off its darkened walls. The furniture, which had also been designed by Pharaoh, appeared to be an integral part of what were, in truth, habitable sculptures. Several nit-picking critics present were busy searching for a straight line, but even the plumbing pipes undulated.

Suzy's boulder was built around a magnificent spiral staircase. Pearl O'Pearl's rock was a world of sound where even the amplifiers and tape recorders were spherical. Influenced by her father, Pearl O'Pearl was now writing her music on circular staves. Several musicians bent over a black marble table, studying her latest work in progress.

Gorodish, Alba and Strawberry worked their way through Cajun stuffed crab, dim sum and a few pieces of gefilte fish before reaching Strawberry's boulder. Her earlier paintings had disappeared and in their place, elegantly displayed against the dark walls, were oval, round and serpentine white canvases, some concave, others convex, in function of

the particular wall on which they hung. So that
Strawberry might have perfect light, round open-
ings resembling those found in the domes of Turkish baths had been pierced through the rock. To
soften the glare a linen drape, similar to those
used in Renaissance artists' studios, had been provided.

Strawberry was busy studying the details of her
new home when she noticed Horace Perceval III,
who was devouring a turkey leg and smirking at
A, his favorite secretary. Strawberry kissed him.

"I'm celebrating," said Horace Perceval III. "I've
not only reached ten million dollars, but I've pulled
off a sensational deal: I'm buying Norway and leas-
ing it to George Lukas and Steven Spielberg who
are going to shoot their next movie there. After-
ward, I'll sell it to the French as a floating film
studio."

"Not bad," said Strawberry.

"Do you want to see my pyramid?"

"What do you mean, pyramid?"

"Come and see."

They climbed up to Horace Perceval III's boulder
which stood next to a waterfall. In the center of the
boulder was a ball of clear plastic, and inside the
ball was a golden pyramid, its sides twisted into
bizarre shapes by the sheer force of Pharaoh's creative
imagination.

"It's a present from Daddy," said Horace Perceval
III. His secretaries now sat at consoles set inside
bubbles hanging from the ceiling. An enormous

white marble reproduction of the Venus de Milo, its belly carved out to form a sleeping area, served as his bedroom.

"Let's find Pharaoh," said Gorodish who was eager to see more.

"Don't ever call him Pharaoh again," said Horace Perceval III. "His name is now Spheraoh."

"Where is he?" asked Strawberry.

"In his bubble. He's so afraid strangers may defile his new studio that no one but the family is allowed inside. Let's see if he'll make an exception for Gorodish and Alba."

The lock was activated by a numbered code. Inside the light-dappled glass passageway water streamed about them, making them feel strangely fishlike.

The bubble, transparent except for the black section rising above water level, was filled with a soft, surreal light. An exhausted Pharaoh reclined on a pear-shaped divan. He rose to shake Gorodish's hand, then kissed Strawberry and Alba. Next to the divan were drafting tables covered with blueprints and renderings. The studio was absolutely silent, except for the sound of water trickling.

"Would you like to see my pensoir?" asked Pharaoh.

("Huh?" signaled Alba's eyebrows. "Like 'boudoir,' only his is used for thinking," whispered Gorodish.)

Pharaoh pressed a button and another bubble filled with bright-colored cushions rose up out of the floor. They stepped into the bubble and it sank back through the floor and began bobbing along beneath the surface of the water. Inside all was quiet, airy, far removed from the world. Spheraoh was smiling, calm and relaxed.

Later in the evening they joined the other guests. Spheraoh put off being interviewed, for he wanted to attend personally to his guests' pleasure. His idea of personal attention turned out to be nothing but a few friendly smiles: he hated having to respond to compliments. At moments he felt a tug of nostalgia as he searched the crowd for one particular face.

"Where are my paintings?" asked Strawberry.

"On their way to the Whitney Museum," said Horace Perceval III. "I sold them while you were away. The exhibition opens in the spring, and I think they've made plans for a traveling exhibit: Europe, the Far East . . ."

Alba and Gorodish were sampling everything, good and bad, that Los Angeles had to offer. Horace Perceval talked to all the guests, telling them about Pink & Pink. If sometime in the next forty-eight hours a few heavy-hitting clients didn't telephone the newest baby-mogul detective agency for an appointment, then something was definitely wrong in this roundest of worlds.

Sometime later underwater lights in the stream were turned on and the delighted guests watched the mermaids Dr. Breuerfliess had provided as a salute to the host.

The only ones not enjoying the party were a small

group of architects who stood in one corner and made bitter remarks about how the master of the house had wasted his talent.

Thanks to her Nabokovary, Suzy had been granted her doctorate. Strawberry was growing rounder, Dr. Breuerfliess's name was about to appear in every psychoanalytic journal in the world, and Pearl O'Pearl had just agreed to write a new tone-poem for the Boston Symphony. The night hung on, as if not wanting to miss a moment of the party. Gorodish was soaring.

At dawn, the grounds began to empty and soon all that remained was the splendor of Spheraoh's creation, and a few friends of the family. The security detail packed it in. All was silence. A fragile light glimmered in the creek; the massive boulders loomed above it.

Suddenly, a Toyota van came screeching through the gate. At first the Indian chef who was preparing an early breakfast, and who had taken a hit or two more of Bombay Black than usual, thought it a hallucination. He also thought he saw nuns come swarming out of the immaculate vehicle. Two more vans drew up behind the nunmobile.

Obviously masters of the martial arts, and using no unnecessary force, the nuns took less than two minutes to round up Spheraoh, Gorodish, Alba and the others.

The Indian chef invited the mermaids to breakfast after which, armed with his ancestral traditions in all matters sexual, he jousted with them in a thousand different manners until exhaustion set in.

During this time, the Toyotas were heading north, toward Santa Barbara. Of course with so many nuns there was no way to escape, not even when the vans stopped for a red light. At one point Gorodish tried to bull his way out of the van only to find himself immobilized with an armlock.

Leaving the highway, the Toyotas climbed up into the hills behind Santa Barbara, driving through newly planted vineyards before arriving at a beautifully restored Spanish mission.

The name over the entrance read:

OUR LADY OF THE ETERNAL EARTHQUAKE

The Toyotas drew to a stop in front of the church. The plaza was incredibly quiet. An aura of calm surrounded the mission.

Once they reached the refectory the "guests" found themselves being treated more graciously. Coffee was offered but no one would speak to the abductors. Led upstairs into what was obviously a convent, they were shown to a balcony lined with comfortable chairs.

Gorodish felt as if the entire score of the *Goldberg Variations* had just stuck in his throat. From the balcony he could see out over an immense meadow. A stage had been set up at the far end: it held a Steinway. Several thousand people were gathered in the meadow, waiting patiently.

The McCoy Tyner Trio came onstage. Tyner sat

down at the piano, pulled the microphone closer and said, in a voice laden with emotion: "We want to dedicate this number to the lady every jazz musician and fan has got to have in his heart. She may be gone, but she'll always be with us: Vida!"

The audience went wild. For the next six hours, the world's greatest musicians relayed each other onstage, playing sets lasting, minimum, thirty-five minutes. Even the church was swinging. And that was opening day of the First Annual Santa Barbara Jazz Festival.

The audience camped in the meadow; stoves were lit. Gorodish, Alba and the others were shown to rooms in the convent. For the sake of decorum Gorodish was separated from his nymph, who shared a cell with Strawberry.

Since no one had had any rest in the last twenty-four hours, they soon fell asleep. Sometime during the night a nun gently awakened Gorodish, handed him a bathrobe and motioned him to follow her up a narrow spiral stairway to a room in the tower. Gorodish was almost certain he recognized the nun leading him.

She opened a door and Gorodish stepped into a spare, simple cell. Smiling broadly, Tristana turned and introduced him to the mother superior.

"Well," said Gorodish, "I'm glad to see you're alive, Sister Welrod."

"You helped me to withdraw from the secular world," she said. "You even helped make Tristana's predictions come true. From my retreat here in this house of worship I shall continue to serve the cause of jazz. But you must be the only one to know."

Going to a cupboard, Vida took out a small valise and handed it to Gorodish. "The musicians collected this. It was meant for the person who would save me. You've earned it."

"Thanks," said Gorodish. "*I* haven't taken a vow of poverty."

"Of course not," said Sister Welrod. "It wouldn't suit you at all."

"Before I go," said Gorodish, "I'd like to ask Tristana a question."

"Yes?"

Almost embarrassed, Gorodish hesitated. "Does your new . . . vocation . . . allow you to foretell the future?"

"Of course."

"I want to know . . . Alba and I . . . will it last?"

Vida smiled. Tristana concentrated, drops of sweat on her brow. "Yes," she said at last, "if you work at it."

Gorodish kissed Vida and Tristana.

"Come visit us from time to time. Be our guest at the jazz festival each year. And if you ever need moral support, or want to know the best day to embark upon a new enterprise, come to us. You'll always be welcome here."

"We'll meet again," said Gorodish, from the tune by Bill Evans.

On his way back to his cell he stopped to look in on Alba and Strawberry who were asleep in each other's arms. Gorodish kissed his nymph on the lips. She opened her eyes, gave him a Buddah smile, then fell asleep again.

Back in his cell Gorodish took three Valium tablets. The fear that one day he might no longer be worthy of Alba had just entered his soul. If that day ever came he would become a gardener at the Convent of Our Lady of the Eternal Earthquake and ask Vida to shoot one last relic of her past into his heart.

The sun shone into the pagoda. Alba and Gorodish were having breakfast.

"Well, my darling, how do you like America?"

"I think we'll stay," said Gorodish. "The croissants are delicious, the city is vast, the freeways efficient, we're not far from downtown, I think I'll start jogging, I love California wine, the sun, the ocean, the restaurants are excellent, one isn't paralyzed by the weight of the past, the beds are wide enough so that two can sleep comfortably, the beef tastes extraordinary, it's wonderful when the waiters recite the menu so you don't have to ruin your eyes reading and at least you get your money's worth, the cars are sumptuous, you don't have to baby the women. . . . I like it here."

"Me, too," she said. "Let's go surfing."

About the Author

"Delacorta" is the pen name of Daniel Odier, a young Swiss novelist and screenwriter. Born in Geneva in 1945, he studied painting in Rome, received his university degree in Paris, and worked as a music critic for a leading Swiss newspaper before taking off for a tour of Asia, which culminated in a book on Taoism. His first book, THE JOB: *Interviews with William Burroughs*, was published in the United States in 1969. Since then he has published seven novels in France under his real name. Odier's four completed "Delacorta" novels are DIVA, NANA, LUNA, and LOLA. He is currently teaching at the University of Tulsa, where he lives with his wife, the violinist Nell Gotkovsky.